MURDER IN THE AGE
OF ENLIGHTENMENT

RYŪNOSUKE AKUTAGAWA

MURDER IN THE AGE OF ENLIGHTENMENT

Essential Stories

Translated from the Japanese
by Bryan Karetnyk

PUSHKIN PRESS

LONDON

Pushkin Press
71–75 Shelton Street
London WC2H 9JQ

'The Spider's Thread' was first published as 'Kumo
no ito' (蜘蛛の糸) in *Akai tori* (July 1918).
'In a Grove' was first published as 'Yabu no naka'
(藪の中) in *Shinchō* (January 1922).
'Hell Screen' was first published as 'Jigokuhen' (地獄変) serially
in *Ōsaka mainichi shimbun* and *Tōkyō nichi-nichi shimbun* in 1918.
'Murder in the Age of Enlightenment' was first published as
'Kaika no satsujin' (開化の殺人) in *Chūōkōron* (July 1918).
'The General' was first published as 'Shōgun' (将軍) in *Kaizō* (January 1922).
'Madonna in Black' was first published as 'Kokui
seibo' (黒衣聖母) in *Bunshō kurabu* (May 1920).
'Cogwheels' was first published posthumously as
'Haguruma' (歯車) in *Bungei shunjū* (October 1927).

This translation first published by Pushkin Press in 2020

1 3 5 7 9 8 6 4 2

ISBN 13: 978-1-78227-555-8

Frontispiece: © INTERFOTO/Alamy Stock Photo

Typeset by Hewer Text UK Ltd, Edinburgh

Printed and bound in Great Britain by TJ Books Limited,
Padstow, Cornwall on Munken Premium White 80gsm

www.pushkinpress.com

CONTENTS

FOREWORD

THE FIRST SUMMER of Shōwa in 1927 found Ryūnosuke Akutagawa at his house in Tokyo's northern Tabata district. On Saturday 23rd July, a day of lingering heat, the author spent a cheerful luncheon with his wife and three sons before receiving visitors in the afternoon. In the evening he retired to add the finishing touches to a draft of his latest story, a tale of Christ reimagined as a poet, and in the small hours of Sunday, at around one o'clock, as a cooling rain began to fall softly in the garden, he entrusted to his aunt a poem that he had composed during the day. Laced with a characteristically pungent sense of irony, the poem bore the title "Self-Mockery":

> Dewdrop at the tip
> Left glinting as twilight fades:
> My runny nose.

Combining this image of nightfall with an allusion to "The Nose", an early work that drew the notice of the literary establishment and set Akutagawa firmly on the path to renown, the poem casts a glance at once elegiac and wry over the author's brief though luminary career. Indeed, those fleeting lines were to prove his *jisei no ku*, his poem of farewell, for only an hour later, having taken a fatal dose of the barbiturate Veronal, he quit the upstairs study, crept into the futon room and, as he read passages from the Bible, lapsed into unconsciousness and then into death.

When Akutagawa took his life at the age of thirty-five, it put an end to thirteen years of literary endeavour that coincided almost exactly with the reign of the Taishō emperor. Lasting from 1912 until 1926, while the Great War and its aftermath ravaged Europe, and while imperial China and Russia succumbed to revolution, Taishō Japan witnessed a glimmer of democratic liberalism wedged between the Meiji emperor's austere paternalism and the militaristic nationalism that consumed the early Shōwa years. It was a period of great artistic flourishing, yet it was also a turbulent time—one of political and economic instability as well as great social unrest and catastrophic natural disaster. By its end, an increasing vogue for Marxism had given rise in the cultural sphere to a new trend of proletarian literature. This, and a confessional brand of naturalism, the so-called "I-novel", stood as the predominant artistic movements of the era. It was against these trends that Akutagawa, whose kaleidoscopic, tiger-bright prose drew insatiably on the Japanese and Chinese classics, on European modernism, and on Buddhist and Christian scripture, emerged as the archetypal *bunjin*, an artist in the finest and most erudite sense of the word, an aristocrat of letters.

His death, perhaps even more than the passing of the Taishō emperor, came to be regarded as the true end of those volatile years. The Marxists, blind to the horrors lurking in the wings, viewed the event triumphantly as the downfall of bourgeois intellectualism and aestheticism. Others, mindful of the "vague anxiety" of which Akutagawa wrote in his much-publicized suicide note, saw in this fatal act a definitive rejection of that rapidly changing world, poised as it was to take Japan further down the road to territorial expansion and all-out war. Whatever his reasons, whatever our own interpretation, time has secured Akutagawa's legacy: to this day he rightly endures as that famous and tragic era's most quintessential writer, and his fiction remains the most dazzling to be produced during those uncertain years.

B.S.K.

MURDER IN THE AGE
OF ENLIGHTENMENT

THE SPIDER'S THREAD

I.

ONE DAY, BROTHERS and sisters, Lord Buddha Shakyamuni was strolling alone by the banks of the Lotus Pond in Paradise. The blossoms on the pond were each a perfect white pearl, and from their golden centres wafted unceasingly a wondrous fragrance surpassing all description. It must have been morning in Paradise, brothers and sisters.

By and by, Lord Shakyamuni paused at the edge of the pond, and He looked down through the carpet of lotus leaves to behold the scene below. For you see, directly beneath the Lotus Pond in Paradise lay the lower depths of Hell, and as He peered through the crystalline waters, He could see the River of Three Crossings and the Mountain of Needles as clearly as if He were viewing pictures in a peep box.

Soon His eye came to rest on the figure of a man named Kandata, who was writhing around in those hellish depths with all the other sinners. This great robber, this Kandata, had wrought all manner of evil and misdeeds—murder, arson, and more besides. But, for all that, he had, it seemed, performed one single act of kindness in his time. Passing through a deep wood one day, he noticed a tiny spider creeping along the wayside. His instinct was to trample it to death, but, as he raised his foot, he had a sudden change of heart. "No, no," he thought. "Tiny though this creature is, it's still a living thing. To take its life on a whim would be too cruel an act, however you look at it." And so he let it go unharmed.

Lord Shakyamuni recalled, as He looked down on this scene of Hell, that Kandata had saved that spider, and so He decided to reward this singular good deed by rescuing the man from Hell if He could. As chance would have it, He turned to see a heavenly spider spinning a beautiful silver thread atop a lotus leaf with the brilliance of kingfisher jade. Taking the spider's thread carefully in His hand, Lord Shakyamuni lowered it among the pearl-white lotus blossoms, straight down into the far-distant depths of Hell.

2.

There, in the Pond of Blood at the very pit of Hell, Kandata and his fellow sinners kept floating up and sinking back down again. Pitch darkness reigned wherever the eye roamed. The only thing to pierce it was the faint glint of a needle on the awe-inspiring Mountain of Needles—and that only heightened the sense of despair. All around hung a sepulchral silence, and the only sound to break it was the occasional sighing of a sinner. For you see, brothers and sisters, having fallen as far as this, they had already been so wearied by the many tortures of Hell that they no longer had the strength to cry out. And so, even Kandata, great robber though he was, could only thrash around like a dying frog as he choked on the blood of the Pond.

And what should happen then but that Kandata should lift his head up to the sky above the Pond of Blood and see there, amid the pitch-black stillness, a glimmering silver thread gliding stealthily down from the high, high heavens. When Kandata saw it coming straight towards him, he clapped his hands with joy. Surely, if he could just grab hold of it, he could climb his way out of Hell. Perhaps, with a bit of luck, he could even make it all the way to Paradise. No more then would he be driven up the Mountain of Needles or plunged down into the Pond of Blood.

Having formulated his plan, he gripped the spider's thread in both hands and began pulling himself up, higher and higher, with all his might. For the great robber he had once been, this skill in climbing was practically second nature.

However, the journey from Hell to Paradise is one of untold thousands of leagues, and so no matter how Kandata tried, it was no easy task to escape. Up and up he climbed until eventually even he was overcome by weariness and could haul himself no further. He had no choice but to rest awhile, and, as he clung to the thread, he looked down into the depths far below.

Kandata's heroic climb had been worth the effort; the Pond of Blood where he had languished only a short time ago now lay hidden in the black depths. What was more, even the faint glint of the awe-inspiring Mountain of Needles was now far beneath his feet. At this rate, climbing his way out of Hell might prove easier than he had imagined, and so, clasping both hands around the spider's thread, Kandata laughed aloud as he had not done in the many years since coming to this place. "I did it! I'm saved!"

Just then, however, he noticed far below an innumerable company of sinners scrambling up after him, higher and higher, like a column of ants. The sight struck him with such shock and terror that for a moment all he could do was move his eyes and let his mouth hang open like a fool's. It seemed as if the delicate thread would snap from his weight alone—how could it possibly bear that of so many others? If it were to break midway, then he—he himself!—would go plummeting back down into the Hell that he had taken such pains to escape. How horrible it would be! But still, an unbroken chain of sinners kept swarming up the fragile, gleaming thread from the very depths of the pitch-dark Pond of Blood. They were coming in their hundreds, in their thousands! He had to do something right away, or else the thread would snap.

"Now listen here, you sinners!" Kandata roared at them. "This spider's thread is *mine*! Who said *you* could climb up it? Go back! Go back!"

That was the moment when it happened, brothers and sisters. The spider's thread, which until then had been perfectly sturdy, lashed the air, sealing his fate. It broke just at the point where Kandata had been hanging from it. Before he could even cry out, he plunged down, whirling like a spinning top, rushing headlong into the black depths below.

The only thing left behind was the short end of the spider's thread, dangling down from Paradise, glittering faintly in a moonless, starless sky.

3.

As he stood on the bank of the Lotus Pond in Paradise, Lord Buddha Shakyamuni followed everything closely from start to finish. And when at last Kandata sank like a stone into the depths of the Pond of Blood, He resumed his stroll, His countenance now tinged with sorrow. Kandata had meant to save himself alone and, as punishment for his lack of compassion, had fallen back into Hell. How terribly shameful it all must have seemed, brothers and sisters, in the eyes of Lord Shakyamuni.

And yet the lotuses of the Lotus Pond were not in the least perturbed by any of this. Those pearl-white flowers swayed their heads by the feet of Lord Shakyamuni, and from their golden centres wafted unceasingly a wondrous fragrance surpassing all description. It must have been close to noon in Paradise.

IN A GROVE

THE TESTIMONY OF A WOODCUTTER
UNDER QUESTIONING BY THE MAGISTRATE

THAT'S RIGHT, YOUR HONOUR. It was I who found the body. This morning I went out as usual to cut cedar in the mountains overlooking the village, when I came across the body lying in a shady grove. The exact location? A few hundred yards from the Yamashina stage road. An out-of-the-way spot with a few scrub cedars dotted among the bamboo.

The body was lying flat out on its back, dressed in a pale-blue silk robe, and it was wearing one of those elegant peaked black hats they wear in the capital. There was only one stab wound, but the blade had gone straight through his chest. The leaves of bamboo scattered on the ground around the body were stained dark red with blood. No, Your Honour, the bleeding had stopped. The wound looked dry. Yes, and there was a horsefly feeding on it so intently that it didn't even hear me approach.

Did I see a sword or the like? No, not a thing, Your Honour. Just a length of rope by the cedar next to the body. And—that's right, yes, there was a comb there, too. Just those two items. But the grass and the bamboo leaves had been so trampled down that he must have put up a terrific fight before they killed him. How's that, Your Honour? A horse? No, a horse could never have made it into a place like that. There's only thicket between there and the road.

THE TESTIMONY OF AN ITINERANT PRIEST UNDER QUESTIONING BY THE MAGISTRATE

I'm sure I passed the man yesterday, Your Honour. Yesterday at—well, it must have been about noon. Where? It was on the road from Ōsaka Mountain to Yamashina. He was heading towards the checkpoint together with a woman on horseback. She was wearing a wide-brimmed hat with a long veil, so I didn't see her face. All I could see was the colour of her robes—a sort of vermilion with a dark teal lining. The horse was a palomino—and, if I remember rightly, its mane was clipped. How tall was it? Taller than most, but only by a hand. Then again, Your Honour, I'm only a priest and don't know much about these things. The man? Well, he wore a long sword and carried a bow and arrows. I can still see that black-lacquered quiver of his: it must have had more than twenty arrows in it.

Even in my wildest dreams, I should never have imagined that he would meet such a fate. Truly, man's life is evanescent: like the morning dew or a flash of lightning. Oh, what a wretched business. Words desert me.

THE TESTIMONY OF A POLICEMAN UNDER QUESTIONING BY THE MAGISTRATE

The man I arrested, Your Honour? He's without a doubt the notorious bandit Tajōmaru. Granted, when I apprehended him, he'd been thrown by his horse. I found him groaning on the stone bridge at Awataguchi. The time, Your Honour? It was last night, during the first watch. He was wearing the same dark-blue robe and carrying the same embossed sword as when I tried to arrest him last time. Only on this occasion, as you can see, he's somehow managed to get his hands on a bow and arrow. Is that so, Your Honour? Property of the deceased? Well then, Tajōmaru must be the culprit. A bow bound with leather straps, a lacquered quiver and seventeen arrows fletched with hawk's feathers—they must all have been the victim's. Just so, Your Honour. As you say, a palomino horse with a clipped mane. He certainly got what was coming to him, being thrown like that. I found the animal a little past the bridge, grazing by the roadside and trailing its long reins.

Of all the bandits prowling about the capital, this Tajōmaru certainly likes his women. Just last autumn, at the Toribe Temple, two worshippers—a palace servant and her child—were found murdered in the hills behind the statue of Binzuru. Everybody suspected that the crime was his doing. If he did indeed kill the man, then there's no telling what he might have done to that woman on the horse. May it please Your Honour to look into this matter, too.

THE TESTIMONY OF AN OLD WOMAN UNDER QUESTIONING BY THE MAGISTRATE

Yes, that is the body of the man who married my daughter. But he wasn't from the capital, Your Honour. He was a samurai serving in the Wakasa provincial office. His name was Kanazawa no Takehiro and he was twenty-six years old. No, Your Honour, he had such a gentle nature that I can't imagine anyone holding a grudge against him.

My daughter, Your Honour? Her name is Masago and she is nineteen years old. She's as bold as any man, although the only one she's ever known is Takehiro. She has a small oval face with a dark complexion, and a mole at the inner corner of her left eye.

Takehiro left for Wakasa with my daughter yesterday, but what cruel twist of fate could have led to this? There's nothing I can do for my son-in-law now, but what has become of my daughter? I'm sick with worry for her. Please, Your Honour, I beg of you: leave no stone unturned to find her. Oh, how I hate that bandit—that, that Tajōmaru. Not only my son-in-law but my daughter . . . [At this point her words broke off, drowned by a flood of tears.]

* * *

TAJŌMARU'S CONFESSION

Yes, I killed him all right. But I didn't kill the woman. How should I know where she's gone? I don't know any more than you. Now, wait here—you can torture me all you like, but I can't very well tell you what I don't know. Besides, I'm no coward. I'm hardly likely to hide anything from you under the circumstances.

I met the couple yesterday, a little after noon. The moment I set eyes on them, a gust of wind lifted her veil and I caught a glimpse of her face. Just a glimpse, mind you—for no sooner had I seen it than the veil covered it again. Maybe that's why she seemed so perfect—a bodhisattva of a woman. Anyway, I decided there and then that I had to have her, even if it meant killing the man.

Oh, come off it. Killing a man isn't as difficult as you people seem to think it is. At any rate, if you want to rob a man of his woman, it's only natural that you're going to have to kill him. Only, when I do it, I do it with a sword. People like you don't use swords. You gentlemen kill with power, with money, sometimes with words alone—all on the pretence of doing a man a favour. True enough, no blood is shed. He might even live well. But you've killed him all the same. It's hard to say whose sin is greater—yours or mine. [An ironic smile.]

Of course, if you can rob a man of his woman without killing him, so much the better. In fact, that's what I was hoping to do yesterday. But it would have been impossible on the Yamashina road, so I hatched a plan to lure them into the hills.

It was easy. I fell in with them and made up some cock-and-bull story about finding an old burial mound in the hills. When I opened it, I said, it was full of swords and mirrors and all kinds of riches and, to stop anyone else from finding it, I'd buried it all in a shady grove on the far side of the mountain. I told them I was willing to sell it cheap to the right buyer. The man grew more taken with my little tale by the minute. Then—oh, isn't greed a terrible thing? Not even half an hour later, they were leading their horse up the mountain trail with me.

When we reached the spot, I told them that the treasure was buried in the grove and invited them to take a look at it. The man was so consumed by greed that he couldn't refuse, but the woman said she'd wait on the horse. After all, she could see how densely overgrown the place was. As a matter of fact, that was just how I'd planned it. So I led the man into the grove, leaving her behind.

The grove is only bamboo at first. But then, after fifty yards or so, you come to a clearing with some cedars—the perfect spot for what I had in mind. As I pushed on, clearing my way through the thicket, I spouted some nonsense about the treasure being buried under one of the trees. No sooner had the words been spoken than he made a run for the scrawny cedars we could see up ahead. The bamboo soon thinned out and we came to a spot where several cedars stood in a row. I grabbed him there and then and wrestled him to the ground. I could tell he was strong—and what's more, he had a sword—but I had the element of surprise. He didn't stand a chance. I had him tied to one of the trees in no time. Where did I get the rope? A piece of rope's a godsend to a bandit—you never know when you might have to scale a wall. I always carry one on me. Naturally, to stop him calling out, I stuffed his mouth full of bamboo leaves. He didn't give me any more trouble.

Once I'd finished with him, I went to tell the woman that her husband had suddenly fallen ill and wouldn't she come and take a look at him. Need I say that was another master stroke? She took off her hat and let me lead her by the hand into the grove. But as soon as she saw him tied to the tree, she drew a dagger from her breast. I never saw a woman so fierce. If I hadn't been on my guard, she might have got me right in the stomach. I managed to dodge her, but the way she kept slashing at me . . . She could have done some real damage. Still, I am Tajōmaru. One way or another, I eventually managed to knock the dagger out of her hand without having to draw my sword. Even the most spirited woman is nothing without a weapon. At last I could get my hands on her without having to take the man's life.

That's right—without taking the man's life. I didn't mean to kill him after all that. But as I was about to flee the grove, leaving the woman to her tears, she suddenly clung to my arm like one possessed. Between sobs she wailed, "Either you die or he dies . . . One of you must . . . To have two men see and know my shame is a fate worse than death . . ." As she gasped for breath, she said, "I'll belong to whichever one of you survives . . ." I was seized by a wild desire to kill him on the spot. [Grim excitement.]

To hear all this, you gentlemen must think me far crueller than yourselves. But that's because you didn't see the look on her face, because you didn't see the fire that flashed in her eyes. When those eyes met mine, I knew I would make her my wife, even if the god of thunder struck me down. To make her my wife—this was my sole thought and desire. I know what you gentlemen are thinking—and no, it wasn't lust. If lust was all I felt for her, then surely I wouldn't have hesitated to knock her down and flee the scene. Nor would my sword have been smeared with his blood. But the moment I saw those eyes of hers in that shady grove, I resolved not to leave there until he was dead.

Still, I couldn't bring myself to kill him in this cowardly way, and so I untied the rope and challenged him to a sword fight. (The rope I threw aside is the one that was found by the trunk of the cedar.) The man looked furious as he drew his mighty sword, and without so much as a word he launched himself at me in a blind rage. I needn't tell you what the outcome of the fight was. Not until the twenty-third strike did my sword pierce his breast. The twenty-third—please, remember this. Even now, I'm filled with admiration for this fact alone. No other man in the world has lasted even twenty blows with Tajōmaru. [A cheerful laugh.]

As he fell, I lowered my bloodstained sword and turned to the woman. But she was nowhere to be seen. I looked for her among the cedars, but even the bamboo leaves on the ground showed no sign that she'd ever been there. I pricked up my ears, but all I could hear was the death rattle coming from the man's throat.

Perhaps she ran to call for help as soon as the fight began. Weighing the possibility, I began to fear for my life. I grabbed the man's sword along with his bow and arrows and headed straight for the mountain road. There I found the woman's horse still grazing quietly. I'd only waste my breath telling you what happened after that. As for the sword, I threw it away before I reached the capital.

There you have it. So do your worst. I always knew my neck would end up hanging from a tree someday. [A defiant attitude.]

THE PENITENT CONFESSION OF A
WOMAN AT THE KIYOMIZU TEMPLE

. . . After the man in the dark-blue robe had his way with me, he turned to my husband, who was still tied up, and taunted him with laughter. How humiliating it must have been for him! But no matter how he squirmed or struggled, the knots in the rope that bound him only cut deeper into his flesh. Stumbling, I ran to his side. Or, no—I tried to run to him, but the man struck me down with a single blow. That was when it happened. That was when I saw the indescribable gleam in my husband's eyes. Indescribable, it was . . . Even now, the very thought of those eyes is enough to make me shudder. Though my husband couldn't utter a word, in that instant his eyes told me everything. But it was neither anger nor sorrow that I saw flash in them . . . only a cold glimmer of loathing. Struck more by the look in his eyes than by the thief's kick, I let out a cry and fell unconscious.

When at last I regained consciousness, the man in the dark-blue robe was gone. Only my husband was left, still tied to the cedar. With difficulty I raised myself up from the carpet of bamboo leaves and looked into my husband's face, but the expression in his eyes was the same as before—that same cold loathing and unconcealed hatred. How shall I describe what I felt then? Shame, sorrow, anger? I got to my feet and, still reeling, staggered over to him.

"Oh, my husband!" I said. "After what has come to pass, I cannot go on living with you. I am prepared to die here and now. But you—yes, you, too, must die. You have witnessed my shame, and I cannot leave you behind in this knowledge."

To utter these words took all the strength and resolve I had, but on he went, just staring at me in disgust. I felt as though my heart would burst. Mastering myself, I began to scour the grove for my husband's sword, but that bandit must have stolen it. It had disappeared along with his bow and arrows. Happily, though, I found my dagger lying at my feet. I raised the dagger aloft and said once more to my husband:

"So then, allow me to take your life—and I'll follow you directly."

Having heard these words, my husband moved his lips at last. Of course, since his mouth was stuffed full of bamboo leaves, I couldn't hear him speak. But as I watched him, I knew immediately what he was saying. With nothing but contempt for me, he said only: "Do it." As though in a trance, somewhere between dream and reality, I drove the dagger through the breast of his pale-blue robe.

I must have fainted again after that. By the time I came to and realized where I was, my husband, still tied to the tree, had already breathed his last. Across his deathly pale face shone a streak of light from the setting sun, filtered through the bamboo and cedar. Choking back my tears, I unbound him and cast the rope aside. Then—what then became of me? I no longer have the strength to tell it. That I failed to kill myself is obvious. I tried to stab myself in the throat. I tried to drown myself in a pond at the foot of the mountain. I tried so many ways of killing myself, but here I am, still alive, to my shame. [A forlorn smile.] Perhaps, worthless thing that I am, I have been abandoned even by Kannon, by the most compassionate, most merciful bodhisattva. Yet now that I have killed my husband, now that I have been violated by a bandit, what is to become of me? What on earth am I . . . am I to . . . [Sudden violent sobbing.]

THE TESTIMONY OF THE DECEASED'S SPIRIT AS TOLD THROUGH A MEDIUM

. . . After having his way with my wife, the bandit sat down on the ground and tried to comfort her. Naturally, I couldn't speak. And my body was bound to the cedar.

But the whole time I kept signalling to her with my eyes. *Don't believe what he's telling you. No matter what he says, it's a lie.* That's what I tried to tell her, but she just sat there on the bamboo leaves, distressed, staring at her knees. Worse still, she seemed to be listening to him. I writhed in jealousy, but the bandit just carried on with his artful patter. "With your virtue sullied like this, things can no longer be the same with your husband. Wouldn't you rather come and be my wife than stay with a man like that? It's only because I love you that I was so rough with you." Oh, he had some nerve, talking to her like that!

Once those words had been spoken, my wife lifted her face to the bandit as though in a trance. Never had I seen her look more beautiful than she did in that moment. But what do you think my beautiful lady wife, in the presence of her trussed husband, replied to him? Though my sprit now wanders between one life and the next, I cannot bear to recall what she said without a blaze of indignation. "Very well," she said. "Take me wherever you will." [A long pause.]

That was not the end of my wife's sin. If that had been the sum of it, I should not now find myself suffering in this darkness. But as the bandit took her hand and led her, as though she were dreaming, out of the grove, the colour drained from her face and she pointed back at me. "Kill him! So long as he lives, I cannot be with you." She screamed this again and again, as if she had lost her mind. "Kill him!" Even now, these words, like a tempest, threaten to toss me headlong into a black abyss. Have ever such hateful words as these issued from the mouth of a human being? Have ever such damnable words as these touched the ears of a human being? Have ever such . . . [A sudden burst of sneering laughter.] The bandit himself blanched when he heard those words. "Kill him!" my wife kept screaming as she clung to his arm. He just stared at her, answering neither "yes" nor "no". The next thing I knew, he sent her crashing down on top of the bamboo leaves with a single kick. [Another burst of sneering laughter.] Calmly crossing his arms, the bandit turned to look at me.

"What would you have me do with her?" he asked. "Kill her or let her go? Just give me a nod. Kill her?"

For these words alone, I am ready to forgive the bandit his sins. [Again, a long pause.]

Before I had time to consider my answer, my wife shrieked and ran into the depths of the grove. The bandit flew after her but failed even to lay a hand on her sleeve. I watched the scene as though it were some kind of hallucination.

After my wife had absconded, the bandit picked up my sword along with my bow and arrows, and made a single cut in the rope. "Now my time has come," I remember hearing him mutter as he ran out of the grove. Everything was quiet after that. Or, no—I could hear somebody crying. As I undid the rope binding me, I trained my ears, until at last I realized that the one crying was me. [A third long pause.]

I finally hauled my exhausted body up from the foot of the cedar. Before me glinted the dagger that my wife had dropped. I picked it up and thrust it into my breast. A mass of blood rose to my mouth, though I felt hardly any pain. Only my chest grew cold, and everything around became even quieter. Oh, but what perfect silence! Not a single bird came to warble in the sky above that shady grove. The sunlight alone lingered among the tall branches of cedar and bamboo. The sunlight—but that, too, gradually faded, and with it the cedars and bamboo. As I lay there, I was enveloped by a deep silence.

Then somebody crept up on me. I tried to see who it was, but darkness was gathering all around me. Somebody . . . That somebody, with an invisible hand, gently pulled out the dagger from my chest. Once more, a rush of blood welled in my mouth. And with that, I lapsed for all eternity into the darkness between lives . . .

HELL SCREEN

I DARESAY THERE HAS never been a man like our great Lord of Horikawa, nor shall there be another. Before His Lordship was born, Her Maternal Ladyship beheld in a dream the Conqueror of Death—or so it is said. Whatever the truth of the matter, His Lordship has been distinguished from birth by qualities quite unlike those of any ordinary man. And that is why we have never ceased to marvel at His Lordship's many and diverse accomplishments. One need only glance at his mansion in the capital's Horikawa district to intuit the boldness of its conception. Its . . . How can I describe it? Its splendour, its heroic scale are far beyond the reach of such unexceptional minds as ours. Some doubted the great lord's wisdom in undertaking such a project, comparing His Lordship to the First Emperor of China or to the Sui emperor Yang; but are not such critics like the proverbial blind men who appraised the elephant by only the parts that they could feel? Never was it His Lordship's intention to court splendour and glory for himself alone. Indeed, he always bore in mind even the lowliest of his subjects and was given to sharing his pleasures, so to speak, with everyone under heaven. Such was the measure of His Lordship's magnanimity.

Surely this is why His Lordship came to no harm even when he happened across the midnight procession of demons at the crossing of the Nijō and Ōmiya Avenues in the south-east of the capital; it is also why, when rumour had it that the ghost of Tōru, Minister of the Left, was seen night after night at his ruined mansion by the river in Higashi-Sanjō—you must know it, for it was where the minister recreated the majestic scenery of Shiogama in his garden—it took no more than a rebuke from His Lordship to make the apparition vanish. In light of such resplendent majesty, it is little wonder that throughout the capital men and women, both young and old, revered him as a living incarnation of the Buddha. It was even said that at one time or another His Lordship was returning home from a plum-blossom banquet at the Imperial Palace when an ox pulling his carriage broke free and injured an old man who happened to be passing. The old man clapped his palms together reverently and offered up humble thanks for having been gored by His Lordship's ox.

So very many tales about His Lordship's life have become the stuff of legend. At a New Year's banquet, His Imperial Majesty once bestowed on His Lordship the gift of thirty white steeds. Another time, amid fears that the construction of the Nagara Bridge at Osaka was counter to the divine will of the local deity, His Lordship offered up a favourite boy attendant as a human sacrifice to be buried under the foundation stone of one of the pillars. And then there was the time that His Lordship, in need of having a tumour cut from his thigh, summoned a monk from Cathay, who knew the art of Hua Tuo. To enumerate every one of them would be a task without end. But of all these great many tales, none inspires more awe and terror than that of the folding screen depicting scenes of Hell, which is now a priceless treasure of that most noble family. Even His Lordship, ordinarily so imperturbable, was greatly shocked by what happened, and for those of us who waited upon him—well, need it be said that it robbed us of our breath? In all my twenty years in His Lordship's service, never again did I witness such horrors as that.

In order to tell the story of the Hell screen, however, I must first tell you of an artist called Yoshihide, for he was the man who created it.

2.

Doubtless there will be those alive today who still recall the name Yoshihide. So great was his renown that it was said no other painter in those days could compare to him. Back then he must have been approaching fifty years of age, and, to look at him, he was only a mean-spirited little old man, all skin and bones. When making his appearance at His Lordship's mansion, he would dress decorously enough, often garbed in fine clove-coloured silk robes with broad sleeves and a tall soft black hat, but his person, his character, left much to be desired. You could see it in his conspicuously red lips, so unnatural in a man of his years, which imbued him with a sinister, almost bestial look. Some said that the scarlet came from moistening his artist's brush with his lips, but I wonder about that. Crueller tongues liked to say that Yoshihide looked and moved like a monkey, and even gave him the nickname "Monkeyhide".

Why, that very name reminds me of a certain story. Yoshihide had a daughter, you see—a young girl of fifteen, charming and quite unlike her father. She had been taken into the Horikawa mansion as a lady's maid. Perhaps because she had lost her mother at a tender age, the girl was full of compassion and had a maturity and intelligence well beyond her years. Her attentiveness to the needs of others earned her the love and affection of everyone from Her Ladyship down.

It so happened that a man from the province of Tamba presented His Lordship with a tame monkey, and the young master, then at the height of his boyish mischief, named the monkey Yoshihide. The monkey was odd-looking enough as it was, but to bestow on it the name Yoshihide made every last person in the household laugh. Ah, if only they had been content to laugh and leave it at that! But no, whatever the monkey did—be it climbing to the tops of the pine trees in the garden or defiling the tatami mats in the servants' quarters—people would always like to tease it, crying out its name, "Yoshihide! Yoshihide!"

Even so, one day, as Yoshihide's daughter happened to be passing along a long gallery, carrying a letter knotted to a branch of winter plum blossom, the monkey Yoshihide came tearing through a sliding door at the far end. The hirpling creature seemed unable to climb up a post, as it usually did when it was frightened. Who then should appear in pursuit of it but the young master himself, brandishing a switch and shouting: "Come back, you tangerine thief! Come back!" Seeing this, Yoshihide's daughter was about to retreat, but the monkey clung to the hem of her robes with a plaintive cry. The girl must have been moved by sudden pity for the creature, for, still holding the plum branch in one hand, she gently scooped up the monkey into the soft folds of her lavender sleeve with the other and, bowing slightly to the young master, said with cool distinction:

"Forgive me, Your Lordship, but he's only an animal. Will it not please you pardon him?"

Still raging from the chase, the young master scowled and stamped his foot several times. "Why are you protecting him?" he demanded. "That monkey's a tangerine thief!"

"He's only an animal, Your Lordship . . ." the girl repeated, before adding with a plaintive smile: "And after all, his name is Yoshihide. I can't very well stand by and watch my father be chastised."

On hearing these words, the young master relented. "Is that so?" he said grudgingly. "Well, since it's your father's life you're pleading for, I'll let him off just this once."

With that, he discarded the switch and stalked off through the sliding door.

3.

Thereafter, Yoshihide's daughter grew close to the monkey. She tied a pretty crimson cord around its neck and hung from it a golden bell that she had received as a gift from Her Ladyship, after which the monkey would never be parted from her side. And when, one day, Yoshihide's daughter was laid up with a cold, the monkey kept watch by her bedside and—was it a trick of my imagination?—wore a forlorn look as it gnawed its nails.

Oddly enough, no one tormented the poor creature after that. On the contrary, they gradually began to dote on it. In the end, even the young master would throw it the occasional chestnut or persimmon, and I heard that he once flew into a terrible rage when one of his retainers kicked it. Afterwards, His Lordship ordered Yoshihide's daughter to appear before him with the monkey in her arms, for he had heard about the young master's tantrum. (Naturally, he had also heard stories of the girl's love for the monkey.)

"Your filial piety is admirable," he told the girl and, in recognition of this, presented her with a fine scarlet underrobe. I am told that His Lordship was especially gratified when the monkey, imitating the girl as she received the gift, bowed reverently before him with its arms aloft. And so the favour that His Lordship bestowed on Yoshihide's daughter was born of a wish to reward her filial piety and the kindness she had shown the monkey, and not, as was widely rumoured, because of his sybaritic tendencies. True, such gossip was not entirely unfounded, but there is time enough to tell you all that later. For now, suffice it to say that His Lordship was not the sort of man who would lavish his affections on the daughter of a lowly painter, however beautiful she might be.

And so, thus raised in His Lordship's esteem, Yoshihide's daughter respectfully withdrew, but, wise thing that she was, she was careful not to let this event draw the envy of other, less modest, ladies-in-waiting. Quite the opposite, in fact: they grew ever fonder of Yoshihide's daughter and the monkey, and Her Ladyship would not let the pair leave her side, even taking them with her in her ox-drawn carriage when she went to observe religious rites at the shrines and so forth.

But let us leave the girl for now and return to her father, Yoshihide. You see, while the monkey soon enough became the darling of the household, the real Yoshihide remained a figure of common contempt, and behind his back they continued to call him Monkeyhide. And not only in the Horikawa mansion. Even His Eminence the Prelate of Yokawa detested

Yoshihide to such a degree that the very mention of him would be enough to turn the prelate's face puce, as if he had come face to face with a devil. (True, some said that this was because Yoshihide had painted a number of satirical works, caricaturing the prelate and his conduct, but since this was a rumour that circulated among the lower classes it can hardly be credited with any authority.) In any case, such was Yoshihide's notoriety that you would have heard the same story wherever you enquired. If anyone spoke kindly of him at all, it was only a handful of fellow-artists, or else those who were familiar with Yoshihide's work but not with the man himself.

You see, Yoshihide was despised not only for his appearance. Indeed, he had a number of wicked traits for which people loathed him even more, and so one cannot say that he did not reap what he sowed.

4.

To wit: Yoshihide was miserly, covetous, utterly without shame, bone idle, rapacious—but, worst of all, he was a tremendously proud and arrogant man. Never would he let you forget that he was the greatest painter in the realm. But his arrogance did not limit itself to painting. He would not rest until he had held up to ridicule every last custom and convention held dear by ordinary people. A longstanding apprentice of Yoshihide's told me the following story: one day, at the mansion of a certain gentleman, Yoshihide witnessed the renowned Shamaness of the Cypress Enclosure undergo spirit possession. The oracle delivered a terrifying message from the spirit, but, having none of it, Yoshihide took up a handy brush and set about carefully reproducing the woman's awesome face in ink, as though he viewed the spirit possession as nothing more than a puerile trick.

That is the sort of man that Yoshihide was, and so it should be little wonder that his works contain all manner of sacrilege. In depicting the beautiful and auspicious goddess Kisshōten, he used the face of a common harlot; in depicting the wrathful Fudō in his nimbus of flames, he modelled the god on the figure of a petty criminal who had been paroled to work for the local magistrate. If you tried to rebuke him for this, he would respond with feigned innocence: "Are you trying to tell me that my own buddhas and gods are going to inflict punishment on me for having painted them?" Even his own apprentices were shocked and appalled by these words. Several of them, in fact, fearing their own punishment in the hereafter, hastened to leave his employ ... Put plainly, his arrogance was staggering. After all, the man held himself to be the greatest human being under heaven.

It should therefore go without saying that there was no limit to Yoshihide's esteem for his own artistry. True, his colours and brushwork were utterly unlike those of other painters of the day, and so among his detractors (that is, those fellow painters) he had the reputation of a charlatan. They waxed lyrical over the work of old masters like Kawanari and Kanaoka—saying that on moonlit nights you could actually smell the plum blossoms on a painted door, or that you could really hear the courtier playing his flute on a painted screen—but when their talk turned to Yoshihide's paintings, all they invariably had to say was that they were odd and uncanny. Take, for instance, his depiction of the Five Stages of Rebirth on the Ryūgaiji Temple gate. One person claimed that as you passed through the gate late at night, you could hear the sighs and sobbing of the celestial beings. Another even claimed that he could smell the flesh of the dead rotting. And of the portraits of the ladies-in-waiting commissioned by His Lordship? It was said that every one of them had fallen ill and died within three years, as though, in capturing their likeness, Yoshihide had also taken their soul. According to those who vilified him, this was the final proof that Yoshihide's art was heretical.

But as I have said, Yoshihide was a perverse man, and so he took great pride in remarks like these. When it once pleased His Lordship to joke, "You appear to take pleasure in all manner of unsightly things," Yoshihide's unnaturally red lips creased into an unnerving smile and he replied haughtily, "Yes, My Lord, it's true. Other more frivolous painters lack the insight required to perceive beauty in what offends the eye." He may well have been the greatest painter in the realm, but it amazed me how he could dare spout such boastful nonsense in the presence of His Lordship. It is little wonder that in private that same apprentice of Yoshihide's nicknamed him "Chira Eiju", after the long-nosed goblin who, as you will surely know, made the crossing from ancient Cathay to spread the poison of arrogance.

But even Yoshihide—even this man in all his unspeakable perversity—had an almost humane soft spot when it came to one thing . . .

5.

By this, I mean of course his only daughter, the young lady-in-waiting, whom he loved to distraction. The girl, as I have already mentioned, was the most kind-hearted creature and utterly devoted to her father, and her love was matched every bit by his. Indeed, this man, who never gave alms at any temple, spared no expense in providing for the girl's every need—every robe and hair ornament—so freely and ungrudgingly that there will doubtless be those who refuse to believe it.

Yoshihide's love for his daughter, however, was so pure that never, even in his dreams, did it occur to him to find her a good husband. Far from it: if anyone made improper advances on her, he did not find it beneath his dignity to hire some street thugs to put paid to their efforts. So Yoshihide was far from pleased when the girl took up the honour of being junior lady-in-waiting at the Horikawa mansion, and for a certain time he wore only a look of bitterness in His Lordship's presence. I daresay that those who witnessed this were in large part responsible for those rumours that His Lordship had been so captivated by the girl's beauty that he had sent for her in spite of her father's objections.

While those rumours were entirely false, it is nevertheless true that for fierce love of his daughter

Yoshihide kept praying that she would be released from service at the Horikawa mansion. I remember when His Lordship commissioned a painting of Monju as a child. Yoshihide used one of His Lordship's favourite boys as the sitter, and so splendid was the artistry that His Lordship, exceedingly satisfied with the work, found fit to express his gratitude: "You may claim anything you like as your reward. Just name it."

So what do you think Yoshihide asked for as he prostrated himself before His Lordship? Yes, indeed: he had the presumptuousness to ask that his daughter be returned to him. Where does one find such audacity? To ask that his beloved daughter be released from honourable service in any other mansion would have been one thing, but to ask it of the great Lord of Horikawa himself! It was sheer insolence. Even a man of such great magnanimity as His Lordship could not but feel some small pique of displeasure at a request like this. For several moments, he just beheld Yoshihide's face in silence.

"I cannot allow it," he all but spat out, before standing abruptly and withdrawing. I believe the same scene played out four or five times. Recalling it now, it seems to me that His Lordship's regard for Yoshihide cooled with each re-enactment. The girl, for her part, feared for her father's welfare and could often be seen in the servant's quarters, weeping softly as she bit the sleeve of her robes. This only gave legs to the rumour that His Lordship had fallen for her. Some even said that the commission for the folding screen depicting scenes of Hell in fact came about because the girl had spurned His Lordship's attentions—but that, of course, cannot be so.

As I see it, His Lordship's refusal to release Yoshihide's daughter was born entirely of pity for the girl's circumstances. I believe that, rather than give the girl up to an obstinate father, His Lordship graciously saw fit to keep her in the Horikawa mansion, where she should want for nothing. There can be no doubt, of course, that His Lordship was well disposed towards this sweet-tempered girl; however, to aver that his affections were lascivious in any way is a gross misrepresentation. I would even go so far as to call it an outright fabrication.

Thus at any rate did Yoshihide, owing to the matter of his daughter, come to fall out of favour with His Lordship. And yet one day, unexpectedly, His Lordship took it into his mind to summon Yoshihide and commission him to paint a folding screen depicting the tortures of Hell.

6.

The folding screen . . . One need only mention it and even now I can see before me those terrifying scenes of Hell in every detail.

Other artists may have painted similar such Hell screens, but their works were nothing at all like Yoshihide's. In a small corner on one of the panels, he had painted the Ten Kings of Hell and their retainers, while the rest of the leaf was enveloped in a firestorm so fierce that you thought it would consume the Mountain of Swords and the Forest of Blades. Besides the Chinese-looking costumes of the judges in indigo-flecked yellow, the eye was drawn inescapably to the flames of searing colour and, dancing wildly among them, the smoke clouds of swirling India ink and sparks of inspired gold dust.

The brushwork alone in this was striking enough, but the scenes of sinners roasting and writhing in the hellfire were unlike those depicted in any other such work. For in that multitude Yoshihide had included sinners drawn from every one of life's stations, from the highest-born nobleman and courtier to the lowest beggar and outcast. A courtier in magnificent ceremonial vestments, a nubile lady-in-waiting in five-layered robes, a Buddhist priest clutching prayer beads and intoning the name of most holy Amida, an apprentice retainer on high wooden clogs, an aristocratic young girl in her finery, a Yin-Yang diviner holding aloft his wand with its plaited paper streamers—to enumerate them all would be an endless task. But there they were, people of every kind, plunged into seething fire and smoke, attended by wardens of Hell with the heads of horses and oxen, driven in every direction like autumn leaves scattered by a great wind. Look at that girl, the one with her hair tangled in a man-catcher and her arms and legs drawn in tighter than a spider's: is she not perhaps a shrine maiden? And that man there, hanging upside-down like a bat, his breast pierced by a lance: surely he must be some newly appointed provincial governor. There was flogging with an iron scourge, crushing under a hundred-ton boulder, pecking by a monstrous bird, grinding in the jaws of a venomous serpent—the methods of torture were as many and diverse as the sinners themselves.

Amid this scene of carnage, however, surely the most horrifying image was that of the carriage plummeting through the air and grazing the Forest of Blades, whose tips thrust up like the tusks of a beast (and where heaps of dead bodies lay speared on the tips of the branches). Blasts of hellwind swept up the rattan blind of the carriage to reveal a young woman so splendidly attired that she might have been taken for a lady of royal lineage or one of His Majesty's own consorts, her long black hair flying upwards in the fire, her white neck flung back as she writhed in agony. The figure of the woman, the blazing carriage—every last detail called forth in the mind the diabolical torments wrought in this Hell of Searing Heat. The sheer horror of the scene at large seemed to be concentrated, as it were, in this one figure. It had all been executed with such inspired genius that one might think a single look enough to hear the woman's terrible screams.

Ah yes, and there's the rub: in order to depict that scene, the dreadful event itself had to occur. For how else could even the great Yoshihide have painted so vividly the tortures of Hell? In exchange for completing the painted screen, Yoshihide met with the cruellest of fates—one that would deprive him of even his own life. One might even say that the Hell of this painting was the same one into which Yoshihide himself, the greatest painter in the realm, was doomed in time to plunge . . .

I fear that in my haste to describe to you that rarest of screens, with its many visions of Hell, I may have got ahead of myself. Let us therefore return now to the point at which Yoshihide received the commission from His Lordship to paint the screen and proceed from there.

7.

For five or six months, Yoshihide was so wholly consumed by the commission that not once did he call at the Horikawa mansion. How odd for a man who loved his daughter so dearly to abandon all thought of her after setting to work on the painting. The apprentice that I mentioned earlier claimed that whenever Yoshihide began a new piece, it was as if he was possessed by a fox spirit. Back then, in fact, rumour held that the reason Yoshihide had been able to make such a name for himself in the art of painting was because he had pledged his soul to one of the great deities of fortune. Proof was offered by those who maintained that if you spied on Yoshihide, catching him unawares at work, you could be sure to see fox spirits swarming all around him. At any rate, what was true was that, having taken up his brush, Yoshihide would think of nothing else but the painting's completion. Day and night, he would shut himself away in his studio, out of sight. This painted screen in particular demanded of him, it seems, total immersion in his work.

By this, I do not merely mean to say that Yoshihide would spend his days by the flame of an oil lamp in that room with the latticed shutters pulled down, secretly mixing his paints and posing his apprentices in various costumes so as to draw their likeness one by one. No, that had been his working method long before the folding screen. Why, this was the man who, when painting his *Five Stages of Rebirth* at the Ryūgaiji Temple, went out onto the road and in all serenity sat down beside a corpse—a sight from which any ordinary person would have turned away in disgust—and proceeded to sketch its decomposing face and limbs, down to the very last hair. No matter which words I use, however, there will be those who cannot yet imagine the all-consuming nature of the artist's work. To explain it all in detail would take too long, but I can at least relate the main points for those who care to hear them.

One day an apprentice of Yoshihide's—the one I have mentioned several times before—was dissolving pigments when suddenly his master approached him.

"I think I'll nap awhile," he said. "But, you see, I've been having these terrible dreams of late."

Since there was nothing so unusual about this, the apprentice, while keeping his hands busy, merely answered, "Is that so, sir?"

Yoshihide looked unwontedly downcast, however, and hesitated to make his request:

"Actually it is, and so I wonder whether you wouldn't mind sitting at my bedside while I sleep?"

The apprentice thought it out of character that the master should worry about nightmares and the like, but it was a simple enough request, so he obediently acquiesced.

"Come inside at once, then," said Yoshihide, still looking worried. After a pause he added: "And if any of the other apprentices turn up, you aren't to let them in."

"Inside" meant the room where the master did his painting. That day, as usual, the doors were shut tight, and in the dim light of an oil lamp stood the folding screen, its panels arranged in a semicircle and the images still sketched in charcoal. Yoshihide lay down with his head pillowed on his elbow and slipped into the deep slumber of a man utterly exhausted. Scarcely had half an hour passed, however, when an indescribable, eerie sound reached the apprentice's ears.

8.

To begin with, it was just a sound, but soon, in snatches, the voice gradually began to form words—like a drowning man, groaning and choking in the water.

"What?" the voice said. "You want me to go with you? ... But where? ... Go where? ... To Hell? To the Hell of Searing Heat ... Who? ... Who are you? ... Who can you be but—"

The apprentice, dissolving pigments, felt his hands stop of their own accord. Fearfully, searchingly, he peered at the master's face. Not only had the furrowed skin taken on a deathly pallor, but now great beads of perspiration ran down the face, while the mouth, with its parched lips and crooked teeth, gaped wide as if gasping for breath. The youth then saw something move with dizzying speed inside the master's mouth, as though it were being pulled by a string. Just imagine when he realized that it was Yoshihide's tongue! All along, those jagged words had been tripping off that tongue of his.

"Who can you be but ... Yes, it *is* you! I thought it might have been you. What's that? You've come to welcome me? So I should go with you? To Hell? My daughter is ... waiting for me in Hell!"

I am told that the apprentice was then overcome by an uncanny feeling. His eyes seemed to pick out vague, fantastic shadows flitting about the screen, only then to jump out of it. Naturally, the apprentice attempted to rouse Yoshihide at once, reaching out and shaking him with all his might. But still, as though in a trance, the master kept muttering to himself and gave no sign of opening his eyes. Desperate now, the apprentice seized the dish of water he used to clean the brushes and dashed it in the master's face.

"Since she's waiting . . . Let us take this carriage . . . Let us take this carriage and make our way to Hell!"

The moment the water hit him, Yoshihide's voice turned into a strangled moan. At last he opened his eyes and bolted upright, as though pricked by a pin. But still, visions of the spirits and demons he saw in his dream would not abandon him. For several moments, he just stared into the distance, his mouth gaping and his eyes filled with fear. At length, however, he returned to his senses, at which point he barked at the poor apprentice, without a drop of civility:

"I'm fine! Get away from me!"

Knowing that he would receive a terrible scolding if he disobeyed the master at a time like this, the apprentice hurriedly made his exit. And when he emerged to see the bright sunlight once more, he gasped as though it were he himself who had woken from the nightmare.

However, this was by no means Yoshihide at his worst. Only a month later, he called yet another apprentice into his room and there, as he gnawed on his paintbrush by the dim light of the oil lamp, he suddenly turned to the boy and said, "My apologies, but I need you naked again." The master had ordered such things even before then, so the apprentice complied, casting off his clothes immediately. Now, however, as the boy stood there, stark naked, Yoshihide frowned mysteriously.

"I want to see a man bound in chains," he said. "So please do as I say. Forgive me, but it will take some time." There was not a hint of regret in his cold tone.

By nature, the burly youth was more suited to holding a sword than an artist's brush, but even he seemed to take fright at the prospect of this. "I thought the master had gone mad and was planning to kill me," he would say whenever he recounted the story in later years. It seems, however, that Yoshihide was irritated by the lad's dawdling, and so he hauled out a slender iron chain from heaven knows where and all but pounced on the youth's back, wrenching both his arms up behind him and winding the rattling chain about them. Having achieved that, he gave the end of the chain a cruel, sudden yank and sent the apprentice crashing down onto the floor.

9.

In those moments, the apprentice, I am told, looked just like a jug of sake that someone had knocked over.

His arms and legs mercilessly contorted, he could only move his head. And with the chain cutting off his circulation, his body swelled with blood and the skin on his face, his torso—everywhere!—flushed crimson. Yoshihide, however, did not seem especially concerned by this; he just kept circling this sake-jug of a body, observing it from every angle and making sketch upon sketch. Oh, what torture that poor apprentice endured, fettered like that . . . I hardly dare commit it to paper.

The lad's ordeal would surely have gone on longer were it not for what happened next. Fortunately—or should I say unfortunately?—a thin, meandering slick of black oil oozed out from behind an amphora standing in one corner of the room. At first, it moved slowly, very much like a viscous liquid, but then it began to glide along the floor more fluidly, glinting in the darkness, until it slithered right up to the apprentice's nose. He took a good look at it and gasped.

"A snake! A snake!" he cried.

As he recalled, it was at that point that every drop of blood in his veins seemed to freeze. And no wonder: the snake was poised to touch the tip of its cold tongue to the flesh of his neck, just where the chains were biting. For all his perversity, even Yoshihide must have been struck by the full horror of this unforeseeable turn of events. Throwing down his brush in a panic, he stooped and deftly caught the snake by the tail, holding it upside down. As it dangled there, the snake raised its head and began to coil around its own body, but no matter how it tried, it was unable to reach Yoshihide's hand.

"Damn! You ruined a perfectly good brushstroke!" Yoshihide growled at the snake. And just like that, he hurled the snake back into the amphora in the corner. With obvious reluctance, he then undid the chains binding the young apprentice's body. That, however, was all he did, for not so much as a word of kindness for the lad fell from his lips. I expect he was more enraged at having botched a single stroke than he was concerned that his apprentice might be bitten by a snake. It transpired later that Yoshihide had been keeping the snake with the intention of sketching it.

I should imagine that what little you have heard will suffice for you to comprehend the strange manic obsession that was Yoshihide's method. Even so, permit me to give you one last terrifying example. This time, it concerns an apprentice of only thirteen or fourteen, who for the sake of the Hell screen almost lost his life. It happened one night as the unsuspecting boy, whose complexion was as pure and fair as any maiden's, was summoned to the master's room. There he found Yoshihide by the oil lamp, feeding scraps of raw meat from the palm of his hand to a bird, the likes of which he had never before seen. The bird must have been the size of the average cat. Yes, and it had feathers sticking up like ears, and big, round, amber eyes—all this, too, reminded him of a cat.

10.

Yoshihide was the sort of man who could not abide anyone prying into his private affairs. He never told the apprentices—and the snake I just mentioned is a case in point—what sorts of things he had in that room of his. And so, depending on what he was painting at the time, you could be sure to find all manner of unexpected objects there—a skull perching on top of the table one day, and rows of silver bowls and gold-lacquered stands the next. Where on earth he stored all these things, however, no one could say. Surely this must have given rise to the rumour that a great god of fortune had an unseen hand in helping Yoshihide.

So it was that the apprentice, supposing to himself that Yoshihide must have been using that extraordinary bird on the table for the Hell screen, knelt before the artist and asked with due deference:

"How can I be of service, Master?"

Almost as if he had not heard the boy speak, Yoshihide licked his red lips. "How do you like that?" he said, jerking his chin birdward. "Isn't it tame?"

"But what is it, Master?" asked the apprentice, keeping his wary eyes trained on this cat-like bird with ears. "I've never seen a creature like it."

"What? Never?" Yoshihide scoffed. "That's what you get for being raised in the city. It's a horned owl. A hunter brought it to me a few days ago from Mount Kurama. Only, it's rare to find ones so tame."

As he spoke, Yoshihide slowly raised his hand and gave the feathers on the owl's back a soft upward stroke as it gulped down the chunk of meat he had just given it. That was when it happened. The bird suddenly screeched and took to the air. Without warning, it swooped at the boy's face, the talons on both legs outstretched. Had he not quickly shielded his face behind his sleeve, he would doubtless have ended up with more than the few scratches he did suffer. Crying out in fright, he began thrashing his arm about in an attempt to drive the bird away, but this only increased the ferocity of its attack. Beak clacking, the bird swooped at him again. Forgetting the master's presence, the boy ran wildly about the cramped room, trying to escape the bird—now standing to defend himself, now crouching to bat the bird away. The strange creature shadowed him at every step, however, soaring high and diving low with him, using every opening to aim straight for his eyes. Each terrific flap of its beating wings transported the boy. He felt so lost, he said after the ordeal was over, that it was as if the master's room had turned into a ghostly valley buried deep in the mountains. He imagined he could sense all manner of fantastic things—the smell of rotting leaves, the spray of a waterfall, the sour pungency of monkey wine. He even wondered whether the dim glow of the oil lamp was not the moonlight on a misty night. It was all as uncanny as could be.

The owl's assault, however, was not the only thing to frighten the young apprentice. No, what made his hair stand on end far more than that was the sight of the master, who, as he followed the commotion with chilling composure, carefully spread out a sheet of paper and licked the tip of his brush before capturing the terrible spectacle of the maiden-like youth being tormented by this monstrous bird. All it took was the briefest glance for the apprentice to see this, and in an instant he was gripped by indescribable fear. He told me that for a time he wondered whether the master's intent hadn't been to kill him.

II.

And really, you couldn't say that such an idea was wholly out of the question. For it did seem that Yoshihide's sole purpose in summoning the apprentice that night was to set the owl on the boy and paint the scene as he ran around trying to escape it. And so, no sooner had the apprentice glimpsed what the master was doing than he instinctively raised his arms, shielding his face with his sleeves, and let out an incomprehensible scream as he cowered at the foot of the sliding door in the corner of the room. In that same instant, Yoshihide himself let out a panicked cry and was about to jump to his feet when all of a sudden the beating of the owl's wings grew more furious and there was an almighty crash, as if something had toppled over and broken. The apprentice now lifted his arm from his face once again to find the room in total darkness and the master calling angrily for the other apprentices.

At last there came a far-off reply and presently in rushed an apprentice, bearing aloft a lantern. Its sooty-smelling glow revealed that the oil lamp had been knocked over, and that the mats and floorboards were now slicked with oil. The owl, too, now lay on the floor, in apparent pain, frantically flapping one wing. On the far side of the table, Yoshihide had managed to raise himself half up off floor and, with a startled look on his face, sat there, muttering unintelligibly. And little wonder: the pitch-black snake had coiled itself tightly around the owl's body, from the neck down to one of its wings. The apprentice must have overturned the amphora as he cowered in the corner, and when the snake slithered out, the owl must have made the mistake of trying to catch it, initiating all this mayhem. The two apprentices exchanged glances and for the briefest moment only marvelled at this strange spectacle before them. They then bowed silently to the master and slipped out of the room. What happened afterwards to the snake and the bird, no one knows.

There were any number of similar such tales. I neglected to mention that, since it was the start of autumn when His Lordship commissioned Yoshihide to paint the Hell screen, the apprentices had to live right through until the end of winter with the ever-present menace of the master's eccentricities. At the winter's end, however, something happened. Yoshihide's mood darkened and he began to lash out at the assistants. Though only one-fifth of the screen remained incomplete, there was no sign of any further progress. Not only that, but there were times when Yoshihide seemed to be on the verge of painting over what he had already done.

And yet, nobody knew what exactly that something was. Nor did anyone dare try to find out. Schooled by bitter experience, the apprentices felt as though they were locked in a cage with a tiger or a wolf, and they used every trick they could think of to keep their distance from the master.

12.

And so, there is little noteworthy that I can tell you about that period. If I had to say something, it would only be to observe that for some strange reason the stubborn old man had grown tearful, and people said that he would often weep whenever he was alone. I heard from an apprentice that one day, when he went into the garden to fetch something, he saw the master standing in the gallery, idly gazing up at the spring sky as his eyes filled with tears. Embarrassed for the old man, the boy turned silently and slipped away. But how odd that this arrogant man, that he, who for his *Five Stages of Rebirth* went so far as to sketch a corpse by the side of the road, should cry like a child just because the painting of a folding screen wasn't going as well as he wanted?

Even so, Yoshihide worked busily a day on the screen, obsessed almost to the point of madness. Yet, all the while, his daughter grew more and more melancholy, until even we began to notice that she was choking back tears. Pale skinned and demure, she had always had a pathetic look about her, but now, as her eyelashes grew heavy and dark shadows formed about her eyes, she looked positively wretched. At first, there was all manner of speculation: we thought she might be worried about her father, or perhaps suffering the pangs of love. But then came talk that it was all because His Lordship was trying to bend her to his will. Only after that did the rumours stop, as if everybody had suddenly forgotten about her.

It was around then that a certain incident occurred. One night, well after the first watch, I was walking alone down the gallery, when all of a sudden the monkey Yoshihide came flying at me and started pulling at my trouser legs. As I recall, it was a warm night, the sort where you can catch the sweet fragrance of plum blossom in the pale moonlight. But that night, in the moon's dim glow, all I saw was the monkey baring its white fangs, wrinkling its nose and screeching like a madman. An eerie chill was only three parts of what I felt: the remaining seven were taken up by the annoyance I felt at the monkey for pulling at my new trousers. My first thought was to kick the creature aside and continue on my way, but then I remembered the retainer who incurred the young master's displeasure by mistreating the monkey, so I changed my mind. Besides, the way the creature was behaving, it was obvious that something was wrong. In the end, I decided to find out what the matter was and allowed myself to be dragged where the monkey desired to take me.

After turning a corner in the gallery, the animal led me to a spot where I could look out, through the gently drooping branches of some pines, at His Lordship's pond glinting in the moonlight. As soon as I arrived there, however, my ears were assaulted by the frantic yet strangely muffled sounds of what I took to be a struggle in one of the nearby rooms. Everything else was still. The only other sound was that of a fish splashing in the mélange of moonlight and night mist. Thus, I instinctively paused when I heard something going on. If it was an intruder, I resolved, I would show him what for. And so, my breath held, I edged closer to the sliding door.

13.

It seems, however, that my approach was too slow for the monkey's liking. Twice, thrice, it circled my feet impatiently, screeching as though someone were trying to strangle it. Then, without warning, it bounded up onto my shoulder. Instinctively, I craned my neck to one side in order to avoid being scratched by the creature's claws, but the monkey gripped onto my sleeve to keep from falling down. In that instant, I staggered back hitting the door with my full weight. It was impossible to delay another moment. I slung open the door, poised to hurl myself into the room's dark interior, beyond the moonlight's reach. But I was amazed to see a woman blocking my view—or rather, no, coming straight at me like a shot from the depths of the room. She would have collided with me, but for the fact that she dropped to her knees as she came tumbling out. Gasping for breath and trembling, she looked up at me as though she were beholding some terrifying sight.

I am sure I need not tell you that it was Yoshihide's daughter. That night, however, my eyes saw her with a vivid freshness, as though they were looking at an entirely different person. Her eyes were big and sparkling. Her cheeks were aflame with scarlet. And her dishevelled clothes gave her an almost erotic allure that contrasted sharply with her usual childlike innocence. Could this really be Yoshihide's daughter, I wondered. That delicate creature, so unassuming in all things? As

I leant against the sliding door and gazed at the figure of that beautiful girl bathed in moonlight, I heard footsteps hurriedly receding into the distance. Using my eyes alone, I silently asked her: "Who was that?"

Biting her lip, the girl shook her head in silence. There was what seemed to be a profound look of shame written on her face.

I leant in and brought my lips to her ear, whispering the same question aloud. But again, the girl only shook her head without a word of reply. Why, she even bit her lip so hard that tears welled at the tips of her long lashes.

A fool by nature, I fail to grasp even the simplest things, and so I had no idea what to say to her. For some while I just stood there, stock-still, as though straining to hear the pounding of her heart. Then again, was my silence not also caused by a feeling that it would be somehow wrong of me to question her further?

I do not know how long all this went on, but eventually I slid the door shut and glanced back at the girl, who appeared to have regained some of her composure. "Go back to your room now," I said as gently as I could. Plagued by an uneasy feeling that I had witnessed something I was not supposed to, I felt unaccountably ashamed as I carried on my way. I had not even made it

ten steps, however, when I was stopped again by someone timidly pulling at the skirt of my trousers from
behind. I turned around in surprise, and what do you
suppose I saw there?

Looking down, I found the monkey Yoshihide
prostrating itself at my feet. It was touching both
hands to the floor, as human beings do, and bowing its
head over and over in gratitude, its little golden bell
ringing.

14.

Two weeks passed after the events of that evening.
Then one day Yoshihide turned up at the Horikawa
mansion unannounced and requested to see His
Lordship immediately. The artist probably dared do
such a thing in spite of his low rank because he had
long enjoyed His Lordship's special favour. Indeed,
His Lordship was not given to granting audiences
lightly, but that day, as so often, he assented readily to
Yoshihide's request and had him shown in without
delay. As always, Yoshihide had on his clove-coloured
robes and tall black hat. His countenance was more
sullen than usual, but still he prostrated himself with
due deference before His Lordship.

"I have requested this audience, My Lord," he began in a hoarse voice, "to discuss the matter of the screen bearing images of Hell that Your Lordship commissioned. Day and night I have applied myself to the task, surpassing myself in diligence, such that my labours have borne fruit and the work is nearly complete."

"That is excellent news. I am pleased to hear it."

As he pronounced these words, however, His Lordship's voice sounded somewhat subdued and strangely lacking in vitality.

"No, My Lord, I am afraid to say that the news is far from excellent," said Yoshihide, looking a little irritated as he kept his eyes lowered. "The work may be nearly complete, but there is still one section that I have been unable to paint."

"What's this? A section you have been unable to paint?"

"Yes, My Lord. As a rule, I'm unable to paint anything that I haven't seen. Even if I were to succeed in painting such a thing, I should inevitably find fault with the result. And would Your Lordship not agree this is much the same as being unable to paint it?"

His Lordship sneered as he listened to these words.

"Then in order to paint a screen depicting scenes of Hell, you must first see Hell itself?"

"Quite so, My Lord. But a few years ago, during the Great Fire, I saw with my own eyes such fierce flames as one might see in the Hell of Searing Heat. In fact, it was only because of that fire that I was able to paint my *Fudō in Writhing Flames*. Your Lordship is familiar with this painting, I believe."

"But what about the sinners? And the wardens of Hell—surely you haven't seen those?"

His Lordship persisted in asking question after question, as though Yoshihide's words had fallen on deaf ears.

"I have seen a man bound in iron chains," Yoshihide said. "I have made a detailed sketch of another being tormented by a monstrous bird. Thus, it cannot be said that I do not know the tortures that sinners endure. As for the wardens of Hell . . ." here the corners of Yoshihide's lips rose sinisterly, "as for the wardens of Hell, I have seen them any number of times in my dreams and hallucinations. Devils with bulls' heads, with horses heads, with three faces and six arms. Almost every night they come to torment me with their noise-less clapping hands and their voiceless gaping mouths. No . . . They are not what I am unable to paint."

These words must have amazed even His Lordship, for he glared at Yoshihide in open displeasure for a long while. "Well then," he spat, raising his eyebrows menacingly, "what is it you say you are unable to paint?"

15.

"Right in the centre of the screen, I want to paint a nobleman's palm-leaf carriage falling from the sky."

With these words, Yoshihide lifted his head for the first time and fixed His Lordship in his piercing gaze. I had heard it said that, when talking of painting, Yoshihide could appear every bit a madman—and so it was, here and now, that his eyes seemed to take on a truly terrifying expression.

"And in that carriage," Yoshihide continued, "a beguiling noblewoman writhes in agony, her raven hair flying up amid the roaring flames. Perhaps she casts her gaze heavenward, towards the roof of the carriage, her eyebrows contorted as she chokes on the rising clouds of smoke. Perhaps her hands tear at the rattan blind as she struggles to defend herself against the sparks that rain down upon her. Then ten, maybe twenty, fierce birds of prey flock down to circle around her, their terrible beaks clacking. Ah, My Lord, it is this, this noblewoman in the carriage, that I am unable to paint."

"And therefore . . ."

His Lordship appeared to derive a perverse sort of pleasure as he prompted Yoshihide in this manner, but Yoshihide himself, his red lips trembling feverishly, could only repeat, as though in a dream: "This is what I am unable to paint."

Then, snapping all of a sudden, Yoshihide cried out, "I beg Your Lordship, have your men set such a carriage alight for me to see it burn. And, if possible . . ."

For a brief moment His Lordship's face darkened, but then, in a flash, he began to cackle uncontrollably.

"Everything shall be done, just as you ask," he said, still choking with laughter. "Do not needlessly concern yourself with what is 'possible' and what is not."

His Lordship's words filled me with a dreadful sense of foreboding. In fact, his very appearance—white froth gathering at the corners of his mouth, lightning bolts flashing on his brow—was so extraordinary that anyone would have thought that His Lordship had been infected with Yoshihide's own madness. Scarcely had he finished speaking, when laughter—relentless laughter—erupted once again from his throat.

"I'll burn a carriage for you!" he said. "And I'll have a beguiling woman ride in it, dressed in a noblewoman's robes. She'll die an agonizing death as she writhes in the flames and black smoke … I really must salute you, Yoshihide, for only the greatest painter in the realm could have devised such a thing. I salute you!"

Yoshihide paled at these words. For a while only his lips moved, as though gasping for air. Eventually, as if all the muscles in his body had grown limp, he slumped forward, touching both hands to the floor.

"My most humble thanks, My Lord," he said with a show of deference, his voice so quiet as to be practically inaudible.

Perhaps it was only then, when His Lordship spelled it out for him, that Yoshihide perceived the full horror of his plan. In all my days, this was the only time when I found him deserving of pity.

16.

Two or three nights later, His Lordship summoned Yoshihide, as promised, to witness the palm-leaf carriage being burned. He held the event not at the Horikawa mansion, however, but outside the capital, at a mountain retreat commonly known as "The Palace of Melting Snows", which had once belonged to His Lordship's late younger sister.

Heeding His Lordship's command, one of the torch-bearers marched up to the carriage and, reaching out his arm, whipped up the blind. The torch, held high with its crackling flames and quivering scarlet light, brightly illuminated the interior of the carriage to reveal a woman cruelly chained on a matted floor—and oh, who could have failed to recognize her! Her long black hair cascaded gracefully down over a magnificently embroidered silk robe the colour of cherry blossom, while golden hairpins atop her inclining head glittered radiantly. In spite of all the unaccustomed finery, it was impossible to mistake the slight frame, the snowy complexion of the neck—around whose nape a gag was now affixed—or the tragically demure profile: it was none other than Yoshihide's daughter. I could scarcely stop myself from crying out.

Then the time came. The samurai sitting opposite me leapt to his feet and, gripping the hilt of his sword, glared at Yoshihide. In my horror, I turned my gaze to the artist and saw that the scene had driven him half mad. While he had been kneeling on the ground before, now all of a sudden he had sprung to his feet and, with both arms reaching out, was poised to run over to the carriage. Unfortunately, though, as I have already mentioned, he was far off in the shadows, and so I was unable to make out his face clearly. But before

I even had the time to lament this, Yoshihide's face, now drained of colour—or rather, no, not his face, but his whole figure, as though raised aloft by some invisible force—appeared before my eyes with such piercing clarity as cut through the darkness itself. For now His Lordship had given the command: "Burn it!" Whereupon the attendants immediately threw down their torches, and the beautiful palm-leaf carriage with Yoshihide's daughter inside burst into flames.

18.

Fire instantly engulfed the carriage. The purple roof tassels were suddenly swept aside as though in a gust of wind, while clouds of smoke, stark white against the nocturnal blackness, swirled aloft. A shower of sparks then jetted upwards with such terrific force that the rattan blind, the side panels, the gold of the roof fittings, were ripped off all at once in an explosion that sent them flying. Still more horrifying than that, however, was the colour of the flames that licked at the lattice panels of the cabin before shooting up violently into the heavens, as though—if I can put it thus—the sun itself had come crashing down upon the earth, spewing out its celestial fire. As much as I had wanted to cry out before, now it was as if my soul had deserted me and all I could do was look on in dumbstruck horror, my mouth agape at this terrible scene.

But what of Yoshihide? Even now I cannot forget the look on his face in those moments. Instinctively he had wanted to rush towards the carriage, but he had halted as soon as it went up in flames. He stood there motionless, his arms outstretched, his eyes devouring the scene as the carriage was consumed in smoke and fire. His whole body was bathed in firelight, and I could see every feature of his wrinkled, ugly face, all the way to the tip of his beard. Eyes wide-open, lips contorted, the flesh of his cheek twitching continually: inscribed plainly on Yoshihide's face was all the shock, grief and horror that alternated in his heart. I doubt that such a look of anguish would ever be glimpsed on the face of a thief awaiting his beheading or that of the guiltiest sinner before the judgement of the Ten Kings of Hell. Even the strapping samurai turned pale at the sight of this and looked with fear upon His Lordship.

But as he bit down on his lip, smiling sinisterly from time to time, His Lordship stared straight ahead, never drawing his eyes from the burning pyre. As for the girl trapped inside the carriage . . . Alas, I do not think I have the courage to describe to you in detail what she looked like then. The whiteness of her upturned face as she choked on the smoke, her long tangle of black hair as she tried to shake the fire out of it, lastly the splendour of her cherry-blossom robes as they burst into flame before my very eyes—what a truly horrific scene it was. Even more so when suddenly a gust of night wind came rushing down and swept away the smoke to reveal, against a backdrop of scarlet flames dusted with gold, the girl, gnawing at her gag, writhing in an attempt to break the chains that bound her. Truly it was a hair-raising spectacle, as if the tortures of Hell were being staged there for every last one of us to see with his own eyes.

Then another gust of night wind swept through the treetops in the garden—or at least that is what everybody thought it was. The sound came tearing through the dark sky, and suddenly a black object shot like a cannonball from the palace roof directly into the flaming carriage. As the burning lattices splintered, glowing now as though coated in vermilion lacquer, the thing gripped onto the girl's arching back and hurled out, far beyond the pluming smoke, an inexpressibly anguished cry, piercing like the ripping of silk. Another scream followed, and then a third, until, without knowing it, we all found ourselves crying out together. For although it had been left tied up at the

Horikawa mansion, the object we now saw against the fiery backdrop, clinging to the girl's shoulders, was the monkey Yoshihide.

19.

The animal was visible for only the briefest moment, however. A fountain of sparks shot up into the night sky like gold dust mixed in black lacquer, after which not only the monkey but the girl too disappeared at the bottom of a cloud of black smoke. Now in the middle of the garden there was only a carriage of fire, burning with an almighty roar amid raging flames. Or no—perhaps pillar of fire might better describe the terrific blaze that seethed high up into the starry heavens.

Yoshihide presented a wondrous sight as he stood frozen before this pillar of fire. He, who until only a few moments ago, had seemed to be suffering all the tortures of Hell, now stood there, arms folded across his chest as though he had forgotten even the presence of His Lordship, his whole wrinkled face suffused with an inexpressible radiance—the radiance of religious ecstasy. To look at the man, one would never have thought that his eyes were watching his daughter dying in agony, only that the beautiful colours of the flames, and the figure of a girl suffering among them, were a source of immeasurable joy to his heart.

The most curious thing, however, was not that Yoshihide could watch his only daughter's death throes with apparent joy, but that in those moments he was possessed of a mysterious, almost otherworldly majesty, not unlike the rage of the King of Beasts as one might see him in a dream. And was it my imagination, or did the countless night birds, squawking and crying in alarm as they flew around us, frightened by the unexpected fire, keep their distance from his tall black hat? Perhaps even those insentient creatures could see the mysterious majesty that hung nimbus-like above his head.

And that was only the birds. For how much more was it true of the rest of us? Breath bated, trembling inwardly, teeming with a queer sense of adoration, we all, each of us down to the lowliest attendant, trained our eyes on Yoshihide, as though we were witnessing the moment when a lump of wood or stone is transfigured into the holy image of the Buddha. The roar of the carriage flames that filled the heavens; Yoshihide transfixed, captivated by the blaze—what rapture, what solemn majesty! Yet among us only one, His Lordship seated high up on the veranda, looked on as though altered beyond all recognition: pale of face, froth forming at the mouth, both hands gripping the knees of his purple trousers, panting like a beast desperate for water . . .

20.

Word spread far and wide about His Lordship's burning of the carriage that night at the Palace of Melting Snows, and there were many, it seems, who were highly critical of the act. For a start, why had His Lordship found it necessary to burn Yoshihide's daughter alive? The rumour repeated most often held that he did it out of bitterness for his unrequited love. I am certain, however, that His Lordship's intent was to punish the wickedness of an artist who, to paint a folding screen, would go so far as to have a carriage set alight and a human being killed. In fact, I even heard His Lordship say as much himself.

And then there was Yoshihide, who, having witnessed his own daughter burned alive, went on in all callousness to complete the painted screen. This too, it seems, drew much condemnation. There were those who called him a villain, a beast in human disguise, cursing him for having forgotten a father's love for the sake of a painting. Among those who were in agreement with this thinking was His Reverence the Abbot of Yokawa, who was wont to say: "Excel though he may in art, if a man does not remember the Five Virtues, his path can lead only to Hell."

Even so, a month went by and the screen with its images of Hell was finally complete. Yoshihide brought it to the mansion without delay and humbly submitted it for His Lordship's inspection. That day, His Reverence also happened to be at the Horikawa mansion, and I am certain that when he looked at the screen, he must have been shocked by the horror of the firestorm raging though it. Until then he had been scowling at Yoshihide, scrutinizing him from every angle, but now he couldn't help slapping his knee and saying, "Truly masterful work!" I shall never forget the bitter smile on His Lordship's face when he heard those words.

After that, almost no one—at least not in the Horikawa mansion—spoke ill of Yoshihide. Perhaps this was because anyone who viewed the screen, no matter his accustomed loathing for the artist, was struck by the mysteriously solemn sentiment inspired by witnessing the mighty and wondrous tortures of Hell in all their manifest reality.

By then, however, Yoshihide numbered among those who are no longer of this world. The night after he finished the screen, he took a rope and hanged himself from a beam in his room. I suspect that, having dispatched his only daughter to the next world ahead of him, he could no longer bear to go on living in this one as though nothing had happened. To this day, his body lies buried in the ruins of his former home. But now, after so many decades of exposure to wind and rain, the little stone marker will be so coated in moss that no one will be able to tell whose grave it is.

MURDER IN THE AGE
OF ENLIGHTENMENT

W HAT YOU ARE about to read is the last testament of the late Doctor Giichirō Kitabatake (a
pseudonym), which was recently given me to read by
the Viscount Honda (also a pseudonym). Even if I
were to reveal the doctor's real name, I very much
doubt that there is anybody alive today who would
remember him. I myself encountered his name for the
first time only after becoming acquainted with the
viscount, who would relate to me at great length all
manner of tales about life during the early years of the
Emperor Meiji's reign. The following letter reveals
partially and indisputably what sort of a man the
doctor was, and what his character and conduct were.
If I may be so bold, however, I should like to add a few
supplementary details that I learnt quite by chance. In
his day, Doctor Kitabatake was a famed specialist of

internal medicine and, at the same time, a reputed expert on drama, holding certain radical opinions on the reform of the theatre. In fact, it was even said that the doctor himself tried his hand at the art, having once written a comedy in two acts that dramatized the events of the Tokugawa era and reworked material from Voltaire's *Candide*.

In the photograph taken by Tsukuba Kitaniwa, the doctor appears as a gentleman of impressive stature and commanding mien, wearing sidewhiskers in the English fashion. According to the Viscount Honda, not only did his physique surpass that of a European, but he had also been renowned, since his youth, for the exceptional energy with which he undertook every enterprise. Apropos of which, one cannot fail to gain a sense of his character from the handwriting in the letter, written as it is with bold and vivid strokes that recall the wild calligraphy of Zheng Banqiao.

Naturally, I must admit to having allowed myself a degree of poetic licence in preparing this letter for publication. I have, for instance, used the titles viscount and viscountess in accordance with the practice of later years, although at the time there was no such rank. And yet, I can, without hindrance, aver that as far as the spirit of the piece is concerned, the original has been preserved almost to the letter.

*

Most Excellent Lord and Lady Honda,

As I depart this life, I have resolved to confess the damnable secret that has haunted the depths of my soul these past three years, and, in so doing, attempt to unveil before Your Lord and Ladyship my despicable mind. It would of course grant me joy unanticipated if, upon reading this confession, Your Lord and Ladyship were moved by the slightest feeling of compassion for the memory of my person, which by then will have forsaken this world. Be that as it may, if you look upon me and judge me to be a crazed lunatic, if you resolve to condemn me even after death, I shall be in no position to lament it. That the facts I wish to confess are so extraordinary may lend me the slanderous epithet of a madman, yet I beg of you: do not think of me thus. True, these last few months I have suffered terrible insomnia, but my consciousness has remained lucid and, moreover, exceedingly sharp. I implore you to think on our twenty-year acquaintance (I dare not call it friendship) and beseech you not to doubt my psychological well-being. Otherwise this entire confession, in which I attempt to reveal the disgrace of my life, will ultimately be no more than a worthless scrap of paper.

Most Excellent Viscount, Viscountess! I am a dangerous, contemptible man who has not only committed murder in the past, but also plotted to commit that selfsame sin again. What is more, it will surely astonish Your Lord and Ladyship to know that I not only planned but was quite prepared to carry out the murder of someone most dear to you. I pray you permit me to counsel you again that I write in full soundness of mind and that everything recorded herein is the truth and nothing but the truth. Believe me, I beg of you, and do not dismiss these few sheets that constitute my last testament—my life's sole record—as the senseless ravings of a madman.

But I must not waste precious time in talking of the soundness of my mind. The fleeting moments I have left impel me to set down my story, to describe the motives that brought me to commit the murder, the act itself, as well as the strange state that gripped me after the deed was done. And yet—O! and yet—even now, how keenly I am aware of my breath warming the frozen ink, of having placed this sheet of paper before me, and, with fear and trepidation, trying vainly to master myself. After all, to examine my past and set it down in writing means nothing less than to relive a past life. Once more I hatch my plan, once more I commit the deed, once more I am made to suffer the torments of this last year. Can I really have the strength to endure all this? Now I turn to Our Lord Jesus Christ, whom I renounced all those years ago. O Lord, grant me strength.

Since the days of my youth I have been in love with my cousin the Viscountess Honda (forgive me, Viscountess, for referring to you in the third person), who in former years was known as Akiko Kanroji. Should I delve into my memory and enumerate the happy hours that I spent with Akiko? I daren't, lest it impede your reading my letter to the very end. And yet there is one radiant memory about which even now I cannot remain silent, a memory that is forever engrained in the depths of my soul. I was a youth of sixteen at the time, while Akiko was but a girl not yet ten. One fine day in May, Akiko and I were playing under a pergola of wisteria in her family garden. Akiko asked me for how long I could stand on one leg, to which I replied that I couldn't. Whereupon she reached out her left arm and grasped her left big toe, raised her right hand and, keeping her balance, stood like that for a long while. The lilac wisteria swayed overhead, breaking the rays of spring sunlight falling on us. Under the wisteria, quietly, without the slightest movement, Akiko stood stock-still, statue-like. To this day I cannot forget those few minutes with her, so like

a living painting. When I reflect in private, I am aston-
ished to find that even then, on that day when I saw
her standing under the wisteria pergola, I already
loved her in the depths of my heart. Since then, my
love for Akiko has grown more and more intense, she
has forever haunted my thoughts, to the extent that I
very nearly spurned my education. But in the end, I
was so cowardly that I could never even bring myself
to express so much as a word of my innermost feelings. Thus, the months and years passed by, during
which I would now laugh, now cry, under a clouded
sky of changeable emotions. Then, when I turned
twenty-one, my father unexpectedly announced that
he was sending me to faraway London, to study medicine—our family's profession. As I left, I longed to tell
Akiko of my love, but in our family, which holds fast to
austere traditions, it is not the done thing to express
one's feelings openly, and I, having been raised in the
Confucian spirit, feared reproach for any infringe-
ment of propriety, and so I set off for the distant
English capital, bearing in my heart the unbounded
sorrow of parting.

Need I describe how many times during those
three years in England I found myself on the lawn of
Hyde Park, dreaming of Akiko under the lilac wisteria
in that garden of old, or, as I strolled along Pall Mall,

pitying myself, the lonely traveller in a distant land? In those London days it was only the so-called rose-tinted future, the dreams of our coming marriage and life together that even slightly allayed my suffering. Yet, for all that, I returned from England only to learn that Akiko had already married and was now the wife of Kyōhei Mitsumura, the director of the ——th Bank. There and then I resolved to commit suicide, but because of my cowardly nature and because of the Christian faith that I adopted during my sojourn abroad, my hand was regrettably stayed. If only you could have known what grief it caused me! Rather than incur the wrath of my father, I decided ten days after my return to make for London once again. My state of mind then was such that a Japan without Akiko had become utterly foreign to me. Rather than eke out the existence of a broken man in a country that was no longer my own, I thought it better to take a volume of *Childe Harold*, travel to some remote, distant place and, having roamed the world in lonely solitude, bury my bones in the soil of some foreign land. In the end, however, personal circumstances compelled me to abandon my plan to return to England. Not only that, but I began the arduous work of treating the innumerable patients in my father's hospital, who in view of my recent return from abroad preferred me to the other doctors. And so, from morning till night, from one day to the next, I was chained to this tedious post.

At this point, I turned to God to console my lovelorn heart. It was around the same time that I made an unforgettable acquaintance, that of the English missionary Mr Henry Townsend, who was living then in Tsukiji. It was solely as a result of his explanation of several chapters of the Bible that my love for Akiko, after a long and arduous struggle, gradually transformed into a brotherly feeling that was both ardent and at the same time serene. I remember how we would often discuss God, God's love, and man's love for fellow man, well into the night, and how after midnight I would make the solitary journey home through Tsukiji's foreign settlement. My juvenile sentimentality may well provoke your derision, but, I do not mind telling you, as I looked up at the crescent moon over Tsukiji, I would pray inwardly to God for the happiness of my cousin Akiko and weep uncontrollably, overcome by emotion.

I lacked both the courage and the composure to ascertain whether this new turning point in my love had been occasioned, as it were, by my "acceptance of fate" or by some other reason. Yet there was one thing of which I was certain: that this feeling of brotherly love was healing my heartache. With this, for the first time since arriving back in Japan, I, who had feared to receive any news of Akiko and her husband, now began to hope for a closer acquaintance with them. Ah, but what folly it was to believe that my suffering would end and a calm descend over me when I beheld their wedded bliss with my own eyes.

It was this belief that led me in the end to Akiko's husband, Kyōhei Mitsumura. Our first meeting took place on 3rd August, in the eleventh year of Meiji, at a firework display near the Ryōgoku Bridge. We were introduced through a mutual acquaintance and spent the pleasure of that first evening together in the company of ten geisha at the Manpachi restaurant in Yanagibashi. Pleasure . . . Was it truly a pleasure? No, I dare say that pain far outstripped any pleasure. The entry in my diary reads:

When I remember that Akiko is married to this lowlife, this wretched miscreant Mitsumura, it makes my skin crawl and me want to vomit. The Good Lord has taught me to look upon Akiko as a sister; but how could He deliver my sister into the hands of such a beast? No, I can no longer endure the whims of a cruel, wicked, deceitful God. How could anyone look heavenward and speak the Lord's name, when a wife and sister has suffered the affront of being entrusted to such a vile ogre!

Henceforth I shall no longer depend on the will of God. With my own hands I shall rescue my sister Akiko from the clutches of this sexual maniac.

As I write this confession, I cannot suppress the damned spectacle that once again so vividly arises before my eyes. Again I see that bluish mist over the water, those thousands of red lanterns lining the streets, those never-ending rows of opulent pleasure boats nestling against one another. As long as I live, I shall never forget that night, the flashes of fireworks that lit up half the night sky, nor shall I forget that drunken pig Mitsumura making a show of himself in the gallery of the restaurant, crooning unbearably lewd songs, holding an older geisha close on his right and attended by a child geisha on his left. No, no . . . To this very day I cannot forget even the entwining three-*myōga* crest on his fine black-silk *haori*. Have mercy . . . It was on that evening, as we watched the fireworks from the restaurant, that I first entertained the idea of killing him. Lord, have mercy . . . From the outset, my motive for murder was not jealousy, pure and simple, but rather a moral indignation that drove me to punish immorality and root out injustice.

Thereafter I concealed my heart and began to watch Mitsumura in order to determine whether or not he truly was the perverted miscreant that I observed that night. I had the good fortune to be assisted in this endeavour by a couple of reporters in my acquaintance. They informed me of such terrible goings-on, goings-on that attested to Mitsumura's moral depravity, that it was difficult at times to credit them. It was also around then, in fact, that I heard from my old friend and teacher Ryūhoku Narushima that in a Gion brothel Mitsumura had deflowered an apprentice geisha—a mere child!—in consequence of which she eventually died. And still, this scoundrel of a husband dared to treat his wife Akiko, the very image of gentle maidenhood, like a servant. A plague upon mankind—that is how he ought to have been regarded. By then I knew that his very existence was a corrupting force, and that his destruction would benefit the venerable and bestow mercy upon the young. This being so, my desire to kill him gradually developed into a concrete plan.

Even so, I wavered, hesitating to realize this plan of mine. In those perilous days, Fate drew me happily— or, then again, was it not unhappily?—to my young friend the Viscount Honda. One evening, at the Kashiwaya teahouse in the Bokujō district, on the eastern bank of the Sumida river, I heard from his lips a sorrowful tale. I learnt for the first time that he and

Akiko had been engaged to be married, until, that was, Mitsumura, with the mighty weight of gold, forced the engagement to be broken off. Was there no end to my heart's growing indignation? That evening, as the Viscount Honda and I drank by the dim light of a single candle in a room at the teahouse, with its gaily coloured rattan blinds, we poured scorn on Mitsumura, and even now I cannot recall what I learnt without its making my skin crawl. And yet at the same time I remember, as clearly as though it were yesterday, how as I returned home from the teahouse that night by rickshaw I thought of Viscount Honda and Akiko's broken engagement, and, as I did, I experienced a kind of indescribable sorrow. Please allow me once again to refer you to my diary:

After this evening's meeting with Viscount Honda, I am more and more convinced that I must kill Mitsumura in the coming days. Judging by the viscount's intimations, not only were he and Akiko engaged to be married, but it seems that they also truly love one another. (Only now do I see that this is why the viscount has remained a bachelor.) Moreover, if I kill Mitsumura, then nothing will stand in the way of the viscount and Akiko's marriage. It cannot be a coincidence that after all their espoused life Akiko has still not given Mitsumura a child; it is as if Providence is aiding and abetting me. As I muse how,

*in killing this monster of a man, I shall help my beloved
viscount and Akiko to begin at last a happy life together, I
cannot prevent a smile forming around my lips.*

And so now I turn to the execution of my plan. After
long deliberations and meticulous planning, I finally
settled on a suitable place and means by which to kill
Mitsumura. I need hardly attempt to describe in detail
the where and the what of it all. Do you recall the
night of 12th June, in the twelfth year of Meiji, when
His Highness, the grandson of the German Kaiser,
paid a visit to the Shintomi-za theatre? And do you
recall that on that same night Mitsumura, as he was
returning home from that very theatre, took unexpectedly ill in his carriage and died? Well, I think it will
suffice if I tell you that a certain doctor in the prime of
life, who also was attending the theatre that evening,
brought to Mitsumura's attention the unhealthy pallor
of his complexion and encouraged him to take a
pill . . . Oh, may it please you imagine the face of that
doctor. Bathed in the crimson light of hundreds of
paper lanterns, he stood by the entrance to the
Shintomi-za, watching as Mitsumura's carriage raced
off amid the downpour. His soul thronged with the
resentments of yesterday and the joys of tomorrow,
and from his lips issued now laughter, now

sobbing—so overwhelming was it that he almost forgot where he was and how much time had passed. Know, moreover, that when, laughing and crying like a madman, he set off home, trudging through mud and desolate rain, his lips never ceased whispering one and the same name: Akiko . . .

I did not sleep at all last night. I passed the hours pacing around my study. Is it joy that I feel? Is it sorrow? I cannot tell. Some unspeakably intense emotion grips my entire being, and not for a moment has it given me peace. A bottle of champagne stands on my desk. Beside it, a vase of roses. And next to that, a box of those very pills. It is almost as if I am to share my curious repast with the angels and the devil . . .

Never have I experienced such happy days as during those few months that followed. Just as I predicted, the police coroner announced that Mitsumura had died following a cerebral haemorrhage. Soon, in the darkness, six feet underground, his rotting flesh would be feeding worms and maggots. Who now would look upon me and suspect me of the murder? What was more, rumour had it that Akiko, in consequence of her husband's death, had gained a new lease of life. With a face bearing the mark of total joy and satisfaction I continued to examine my patients, and in my spare time I would enjoy seeing the plays at the Shintomi-za—with the Viscount Honda, no less. For me, this was, in faith, my ultimate victory: little more than the curious desire to gaze again and again upon the gas-lit chandelier and the red upholstery of the boxes as though it were a glorious field of battle.

Truly, this happiness lasted for a number of months. As the time passed, however, little by little I inched closer to the most despicable temptation of my life, and to a destiny with which I would ultimately have to reckon. By no means do I have the courage to recount how fierce was the battle I had to fight, how step by step it pursued me to the brink of death. No, even now, as I inscribe these lines, I must enter into mortal combat with this hydra of temptation. If you wish to see the mark of my agony, then may it please you look at the following extracts from my diary:

——th October. *It is said that, since she has no children, Akiko is to leave the Mitsumura house. Viscount Honda and I have decided to pay her a visit in the coming days. It will be the first time that I have seen her in six years. Since returning from England, never once have I met her. This was for my own sake at first, later for hers, and so it has dragged on to this day. Will Akiko's eyes shine as brightly as they did those six years ago?*

——th October. *I stopped by Viscount Honda's today, so that we could pay our first visit to Akiko. I was shocked, however, to learn that the viscount had beaten me to it, having paid her several visits already. Why should the viscount want to exclude me in this way? Feeling terribly awkward, I alluded to the need to examine a patient, made my excuses and left in a hurry. The viscount likely visited Akiko by himself in the wake of my departure.*

——st November. *Viscount Honda and I paid Akiko a visit. Her beauty has faded somewhat, but still, looking at her, it is not difficult to recall the vivid memory of that young girl standing under the lilac wisteria. Ah, how long have I waited to set eyes on her again? What, then, is this implacable grief that I feel in my heart? My suffering increases by not knowing.*

——th December. *The viscount clearly intends to marry Akiko. Thus, my aim in killing Akiko's husband will soon be achieved. And yet . . . and yet, a strange feeling of cruel torment will not leave me, as though I am losing Akiko once more.*

——th March. *It is said that the viscount's wedding to Akiko has been set for the end of this year. I pray that it happen as soon as possible. Otherwise, I shall never be able to free myself of this relentless torment.*

12th June. *I betook myself, alone, to the Shintomi-za. As I watched the performance, naturally I could not hold back the contented smile of satisfaction that crossed my face as I recalled my victim, who on this very day last year fell prey to my manipulations. And yet, as I returned home from that same seat, I was struck so unexpectedly by thoughts of my motive for the murder that I very nearly lost my way. For whose sake did I kill Mitsumura? For the Viscount Honda's? For Akiko's? Or was it for my own sake, after all? What answer can I give?*

——nd July. *This evening the viscount, Akiko and I set out to watch the floating lanterns being released on the Sumida river. In the lanternlight seeping through the carriage window, Akiko's glittering eyes looked even more beautiful, so much so that I almost forgot about the viscount sitting next to me. But now is not the time to write about such things. When the viscount suddenly began to complain of stomach pains, I reached into my pocket and groped for a box of pills. I froze. Were they really "those pills"? Why did I find myself carrying them this evening? Was it by chance? Oh, how ardently I hope that it was by chance. And yet, to all appearances, chance had nothing to do with it . . .*

——st August. *At home I was joined for dinner by the viscount and Akiko. From the first moment to the last, however, I could not put out of my mind those pills lying at the bottom of my pocket. It seems that deep within my soul there lurks a monster incomprehensible even to myself.*

——th November. *The viscount and Akiko have married at last. I can feel, seething inside me, an indescribable rage directed towards myself. I am reminded of the sense of shame that a soldier fleeing the battlefield must feel for his own cowardice.*

——th December. *The viscount asked me to take a look at him. Akiko was also present. She said that his temperature jumps at night. After examining him, I reassured her that it was nothing more than a cold and returned home directly in order to prepare some medicine for the viscount. Throughout those two hours I was hounded by the dreadful temptation of "those pills".*

——th December. *Last night I was tormented by a nightmare in which I had killed the viscount. I have been unable to shake off an unpleasant feeling all day.*

——rd February. *Ah, at last I have come to the realization: in order not to kill the viscount, I shall have to kill myself. But what of Akiko? . . .*

Most Excellent Viscount, Viscountess! Though these are but extracts from my diary, I am certain that you will understand from them the torments that I suffered day and night. Lest I kill Your Lordship, I must kill myself. I could save myself by killing you, Viscount, but then how could I explain my motive in dispatching Mitsumura? Perhaps I poisoned him in the unconscious hope of achieving my own egotistical aims. If so, that would destroy my character, my conscience, my morals, my principles, leaving nothing behind. Which, of course, would be unendurable. It is better, I believe, to kill oneself than to endure spiritual bankruptcy. Therefore, so as to uphold my character, I have resolved this evening to share in the fate of my erstwhile victim, and for this purpose to avail myself of the box of "those pills".

Now my Lord and Ladyship know the reasons that have led me to end my life. By the time you read this letter, I shall already be little more than a corpse laid out on a bed. And yet, as I face death, it is only because I desire in some small measure to justify myself in your eyes that I have taken upon myself the decision to confess in detail these secrets of my damnable life. If you deem me deserving of scorn, then scorn me; if pity, then pity me. I, who both scorn and pity myself, shall gladly receive your loathing and compassion. And so I must lay down my brush. In a moment I shall order a carriage and set out for the Shintomi-za. Then, when the half-day's programme is over, I shall place several of "those pills" in my mouth and resume my seat in the carriage. Of course, the season is different now, but the fine drizzle will remind me of that rainy season, when the plums were ripening. Thus, just like that pig Mitsumura, I shall gaze through the carriage window at the light from the passing traffic and listen to the desolate night rain drumming on the roof of the carriage, and, as I speed away from the Shintomi-za, I too shall draw my last breath. When Your Lord and Ladyship open tomorrow's newspaper—I daresay before you will have received this letter—you will read that Doctor Giichirō Kitabatake died suddenly in his carriage, as he was returning home from the theatre, and that the cause of death was a cerebral haemorrhage.

In praying for your good health and happiness, I remain,

Forever your devoted servant,

Giichirō Kitabatake

THE GENERAL

1. THE WHITE SASH UNIT

IT WAS THE GREY OF MORNING on 26th November 1904, in the thirty-seventh year of Meiji. The White Sash Unit of the ——th Division's ——th Infantry Regiment was setting out from the northern base of 93-Hill to capture the fort at Mount Songshu.

Since the road followed the shelter of the elevation, the unit marched that day in a special formation of four columns. As the soldiers quietly made their way along the barren, twilit path, with their rifle barrels in neat rows and only the white of their sashes showing, they presented a gallant, if tragic, spectacle. Since taking up his place at the head of the unit, the commanding officer, Captain M——, looked much altered: he had grown taciturn, and his face had taken on a subdued expression. The men, however, despite expectations, were keeping up their usual good cheer.

This, no doubt, had something to do with the strength of Japanese spirit.

After continuing to march for some time, the unit emerged from the rocky shelter of the hill onto the windswept flat of a dry riverbed.

"Hey, look behind you!" The man who spoke these words was Private First-Class Taguchi, a former paper merchant. He was addressing Private First-Class Horio, a former carpenter who had been drafted from the same platoon. "They're saluting us."

Private Horio glanced around. Sure enough, on top of the hill, which loomed a deep black against the reddening sky, the colonel and several officers were giving a farewell salute to the men marching towards their death.

"How do you like that?" Taguchi said. "Isn't that something! What an honour to belong to the White Sashes."

"Some honour . . ." replied Horio bitterly, as he adjusted his rifle over his shoulder. "We're going to our death. Then again, if you can buy a life with honour and a salute . . . That's some bargain."

"No, you mustn't speak like that. It's an insult to the Emperor!"

"You idiot! Insult or no insult, what's the difference? A salute won't even buy you a cup of sake in the mess."

Taguchi pressed his lips firmly shut, for he knew well how his comrade inclined towards cynicism whenever he had been drinking. But Horio kept on going:

"Oh, no, they don't say they're buying you with a salute. They make it all sound so grand, so noble. Your country, they say; the Emperor, they say. But it's all a pack of lies. Isn't that just the way of it, my friend?"

The man whom Horio was addressing was the rather docile Lance Corporal Egi, a former primary school teacher who had also been drafted from the same platoon. On this occasion, however, the ordinarily quiet lance corporal suddenly snapped. He shot Horio a menacing look and threw a sharp reply in his comrade's face, which reeked of alcohol.

"You're a fool! Isn't it our duty to die?"

By then, the White Sashes were already climbing the far bank of the dry riverbed. Seven or eight Chinese mud-plastered huts stood solemnly facing the dawn; high up above their roofs, Mount Songshu, cold and russet with folds the colour of petroleum, met their eyes. Once the unit had passed the village, they broke with their four-column formation and, rifles still slung over their shoulders, began to crawl slowly along the lines of communication towards the enemy position.

Naturally, Lance Corporal Egi was crawling on hands and knees along with the rest of them. "A salute won't buy you a cup of sake in the mess . . ." Horio's words were still ringing in his ears. True to his nature, though, Egi kept his thoughts to himself. And yet, more and more those words gnawed at him. As he crawled like an animal along the frozen path, he contemplated death and war. But not even the faintest glimmer of wisdom came of it. After all, dying was still a wretched business, even if it was for the Emperor. As for war . . . Well, he didn't even hold war to be a crime. Next to war, crime, rooted as it was in private passion, was almost understandable. But war meant one's duty to the Emperor, and nothing else. And yet, he—but no, it was not just he, for more than two thousand men, from every division, had been selected for the White Sash Unit, and they too, whether they liked it or not, would now have to die, carrying out that greatest of duties . . .

"Nice of you to show up! Which regiment?"

Lance Corporal Egi looked around. The unit had reached the assembly point at the foot of Mount Songshu. Soldiers from the other divisions had gathered there already, all wearing khaki uniforms adorned with old-fashioned sashes. It was one of those men who had called out to him—the one sitting on a rock, squeezing a pimple on his cheek in the thin light of morning.

"The ——th."

"Circus, more like."

Lance Corporal Egi's face darkened. He offered no reply to the joke.

Some hours later, shells from both sides began to fly with a ferocious roar over the terrain where these soldiers had taken up their positions. The Japanese naval guns at Lijiatun raised towering clouds of yellow dust on the side of Mount Songshu, and as those great clouds curled upward, the air between them would flash with lilac—a sight that was all the more impressive in daylight.

As they waited for the right moment during the bombardment, the two-thousand-strong White Sash Unit tried as best they could to keep their spirits up: this was their only option if they were not to be crushed by fear.

"They're giving us one hell of a pounding, aren't they?" said Private Horio as he looked up at the sky. No sooner had he said this than a prolonged shrieking once again rent the air overhead. Drawing his neck in instinctively, he called over to Private Taguchi: "Those are the eleven-inch guns!"

Taguchi was holding a handkerchief to his nose to shield himself from the rising clouds of dust. He feigned a smile and stealthily slipped his handkerchief back in his pocket so that his comrade would not notice it. Embroidered around the edges, it was a gift from a geisha he visited regularly. She had given it to him just before he left for the front.

"It has a different sound, doesn't it, the eleven-incher?"

As Taguchi was saying this, he shot to his feet as if he had been caught off-guard. At the same time, the others, seeming to heed some inaudible command, began rising to their feet one after the other. The commanding officer, General N——, accompanied by several chiefs of staff, was solemnly coming their way.

"Cut the racket! Quiet here!" said the general in a gruff voice as he surveyed the position. "Since it's a tight squeeze, there's no need to salute. Now, which regiments were you drafted from?"

Private Taguchi felt the general fix his gaze firmly on him. The general's eyes were enough to make him as bashful as a young girl.

"Sir! The ——th Infantry, sir!"

"I see. Well, then, be sure to give them hell!"

The general shook Taguchi's hand before sharply turning his gaze to Private Horio. Once again extending his right hand, he repeated those same words: "Give them hell, too, my boy!"

As he listened, Private Horio stood stock-still and bolt upright, as if every muscle in his body had turned to steel. In the eyes of the old general, at least, this lent a most favourable impression: broad shoulders, powerful hands, high cheekbones and a ruddy complexion— the very model of a soldier of the Empire. Rooted to the spot, the general thundered:

"Those batteries of theirs may be firing now, but come nightfall you men are going to take that fort. The reserves will then follow suit, and all the remaining forts in the area will be ours. You men must throw yourselves at that fort." As he spoke, the general's voice filled with a rather theatrical pathos. "Understood? On no account are you to stop halfway and fire. Think of your body as a living cannonball and aim yourselves straight at them. That's an order. Remember, I'm depending on you."

The general gripped the private's hand, as though in so doing he wished to convey the gravitas of this "depending". And with that, he walked on.

"Well this is going to be a barrel of laughs, isn't it?" As he watched the general go, Horio shot a sly wink at Taguchi. "Now, fancy that . . . a handshake from the old man himself."

Taguchi smiled wryly. Seeing this, however, Horio was overcome by an unaccountable feeling of guilt, while his comrade's smile struck him as unbecoming.

"Well then," Lance Corporal Egi broke in. "Were you bought for a handshake?"

"Now, now, don't you go impersonating me." This time it was Horio who could not resist a wry smile.

"It makes my blood boil to think that your life is being bought, while here I am, giving mine freely."

"Hear, hear," Taguchi cut in. "We're giving our lives *for our country.*"

"Well, I don't know about that. All I know is that we're giving them. If a bandit pointed a gun at you, what then? You'd give away anything, wouldn't you?"

Dark excitement worked between Lance Corporal Egi's brows.

"That's just it," said Taguchi. "A bandit would say, 'Your money or your life!' Whereas death's our only option. At any rate, if you've no choice in the matter, then isn't it better to die a worthy death?"

Private Horio could still feel the effects of the alcohol. As he listened to these words, a look of disdain for his mild-mannered comrade flashed in his eyes. Was it really as simple as *giving* your life, he mused as he looked up at the sky in wonder. And so it was that he decided to repay the general's handshake that very night: along with the best of them, he would become a human cannonball . . .

That night, a few minutes after eight o'clock, Lance Corporal Egi, having been struck by a hand grenade, lay on the side of Mount Songshu, his whole body charred black. A soldier from the White Sashes, after making his way through the barbed wire, came running up to him, shrieking incoherently. Seeing his fallen comrade, he placed his foot on the chest of the corpse and suddenly erupted in peals of laughter. The noise echoed eerily between the fierce gunfire coming from both sides.

"*Banzai! Nippon Banzai!* The devils have surrendered! The enemy is routing! *Banzai* the ——th Regiment! *Banzai! Banzai!*"

Brandishing his rifle, he carried on shouting like this, heedless of the exploding grenades that rent the darkness before his eyes. These flashes of light revealed a gunshot wound to the head, received in the very midst of the attack and apparently having driven the soldier mad. It was Private First-Class Horio.

2. SPIES

It was the morning of 5th March 1905, in the thirty-eighth year of Meiji. In a darkened room at the head-quarters of the A—— Cavalry Brigade, which was then stationed at Quanshengji, two Chinese were being interrogated. They had just been arrested on suspicion of espionage by a sentry seconded to the A—— Cavalry Brigade from the ——th Regiment.

Even now, the brazier in the low-roofed Chinese house gave off a cheerful warmth, but the gloomy atmosphere of war announced itself in the noise of spurs on the tiled floor, in the colours of the greatcoats draped over the table, indeed in every corner of the room. Some photographs of geisha with their hair done up in a sort of chignon had been tacked neatly to the dusty-smelling white-plaster wall; and there, beside them, were affixed two slender lengths of red Chinese paper bearing lines of poetry. The sight was as comical as it was tragic to behold.

The interrogation was being conducted by a staff officer, who was assisted by an adjutant and an interpreter. The Chinese had provided meticulous answers to every question put to them. In fact, the slightly older-looking one with short whiskers had seemed anxious to explain matters even before the interpreter had time to pose the questions. The articulateness of their answers, however, inspired only antagonism on the part of the staff officer, who desired nothing more than to make spies of them.

"Soldier!" the staff officer called in his nasal voice to the sentry guarding the doorway. This sentry, who had apprehended the two Chinese, was none other than Private First-Class Taguchi of the White Sash Unit. As he stood there with his back to the door's swastika-patterned latticework, Taguchi had been ogling the photographs of the geisha, but the staff officer's voice jolted him out of his reveries.

"Sir!" answered Taguchi at the top of his lungs.

"It was you, was it not, who took these two into custody? At what time did you apprehend them?"

"I was on sentry duty by the northern wall of the village," Taguchi began, as though reading from a script. "The two men were walking towards me on the Mukden Road, coming from the direction of Mukden, when from a tree the commander—"

"How's that now? The commander was in a tree?" The staff officer raised an eyebrow.

"Yes, sir. The commander had climbed up to get a better view. He ordered me to arrest them. Only, when I tried to, that one—yes, sir, the one without whisk-ers—well, all of a sudden he legged it."

"That's it?"

"That's the sum of it, sir, yes."

"Very well."

Flushing, the staff officer's face betrayed a look of considerable disappointment. He directed a question to the interpreter, who, to conceal his boredom, tried to imbue his voice with a little animation.

"If you aren't a spy, then why did you run?"

"Isn't it only natural that we should run if a Japanese soldier suddenly decides to pounce on us?" the other Chinese answered without flinching. His leaden pallor made him look like an opium addict.

"Nevertheless, the road you took is being transformed, even as we speak, into a battlefield. Honest citizens would have no business here . . ."

The adjutant, who happened to speak Chinese, shot a malevolent glance at the pallid face of the Chinese man.

"Oh, but we do. Like I said, we were on our way to Xinmintun to exchange some currency. Look, here are the notes."

The man with whiskers calmly surveyed the officers' faces. The staff officer snorted. He was secretly pleased that the adjutant had been shot down . . .

"Changing paper money, eh? And at the risk of your life?" the adjutant sneered, unwilling to admit defeat. "In any case, we'll have to strip-search them."

As soon as the staff officer's words had been translated, the two men, quite unperturbed, stripped themselves.

"You still have your waistbands on. Take them off and hand them over."

The interpreter, as he received the garments, felt that there was something unclean about the bodily warmth contained by the white cotton. He also discovered in them three thick needles, each one about three inches in length. The staff officer examined them, turning them over again and again in the light of the window. However, apart from the flat heads on which there was a design of plum blossom, there was nothing out of the ordinary about them.

"What are these?"

"I am an acupuncturist," the man with whiskers explained calmly and without hesitation.

"Take off your shoes as well."

The soldiers watched on as almost impassively, without even trying to hide their modesty, the Chinese did what was demanded of them. But while of course they had found nothing in their trousers or jackets, nor did they find anything by way of evidence in their shoes or socks.

"The only thing left is to take their shoes apart," thought the adjutant. He was about to say this to the staff officer, when suddenly, from the neighbouring room, in came the general, followed by the brigade commander and the general staff. The general had just paid a visit to the brigade commander in order to settle something between the adjutant and general staff.

"Russian spies?"

As he asked the question, the general stopped before the Chinese and trained his sharp eyes on their naked forms. (Later, a certain American would make the brazen claim that there was a touch of monomania in the illustrious general's eyes. What's more, he held that in situations like this, the colour of those eyes took on a baleful brilliance.)

The staff officer relayed a brief account of the incident to the general, but all the latter did was nod periodically, as though recollecting something.

"They won't confess, sir. Our only option is to beat it out of them," said the staff officer.

Then, with the hand in which he was clutching a map, the general pointed to the shoes lying on the floor.

"Try taking those shoes apart."

The soles of the shoes were soon torn off, whereupon four or five maps and secret documents that had been sewn into them instantly scattered out onto the floor. When the two Chinese saw this, their faces paled. Maintaining their silence, however, they kept their eyes stubbornly fixed on the floor tiles.

"Just as I thought." Smiling triumphantly, the general looked over his shoulder at the brigade commander. "Still, they did think of the shoes ... Come, have them dress again. It's the first time we've had spies like these."

"Your Excellency's perspicacity astonishes me," said the adjutant with an ingratiating smile as he handed over the evidence of the spies' activities to the commanding officer. It was as if he had forgotten that he himself had noticed the shoes before the general did.

"But since you found nothing on them after you'd stripped them, the shoes were the only place they could have hidden them," said the general, still in good humour. "I suspected the shoes immediately."

The commanding officer was also in a buoyant mood. "It's true, the locals are a rotten lot," he said. "When we first came here, they put out Japanese flags, but when we searched their houses, we usually found them hiding Russian ones."

"Cunning and treacherous, eh?"

"Quite so. It's a tricky situation, sir."

While this conversation was going on, the staff officer was continuing his interrogation of the two

Chinese with the help of the interpreter. Suddenly, turning an ill-tempered face to Private Taguchi, he barked out an order:

"Hey, Soldier! Seeing as you were the one who caught these spies, you can have the honour of killing them as well."

Twenty minutes later, at the edge of a road lying to the south of the village, the two Chinese were sitting by the stump of a dead willow, bound together by their queues. Having fixed his bayonet, Private Taguchi undid their queues, then, taking his rifle, stood behind the younger of the men. Before killing them, however, he wanted at least to warn them of their fate.

"*Ni . . .*" he began, but he didn't know the Chinese for *to kill*. "You're to be killed!"

As though having conspired together, the two Chinese glanced warily at him over their shoulders. Without showing any sign of surprise, they began again to kowtow, each in a different direction. "They're saying goodbye to their hometowns," Private Taguchi thought.

Once they had more or less done with kowtowing, as though having steeled themselves, they calmly stretched out their necks. Private Taguchi raised his rifle over his head. But, seeing their meek resignation, he couldn't bring himself to bayonet them.

"You're to be killed!" he repeated helplessly.

No sooner had he said this than, from the village, a cavalryman on horseback came riding towards them, trailing a cloud of dust.

"Soldier!"

As the cavalryman drew nearer it became clear that it was the sergeant major. When he saw the two Chinese, he reined in his horse and shouted haughtily:

"Spies, eh? Russian spies, I'll bet. Here, let me kill one of them."

Private Taguchi gave a wry smile. "You can have the pair of them if you like."

"My, my! Such generosity!"

The cavalryman jumped nimbly down from his horse. He took his position behind the Chinese and drew the sword hanging from his waist. Just then, the stirring sound of hooves could be heard from the direction of the village. Three officers were approaching. Paying no heed to this, the cavalryman raised his sword high. But before he could strike, the three officers came leisurely riding past. It was the commander in chief! The cavalryman and Private Taguchi both gave the proper salute as they looked up at the general on horseback.

"The Russian spies, eh?" For an instant, a look of monomania flashed in the general's eyes. "Well get on with it! Kill them! Kill them!"

The cavalryman promptly raised his sword aloft and in a single stroke decapitated the younger Chinese. His head went dancing and tumbling down to the stump of the dead willow. Before their eyes, the blood spread out, pooling on the yellow earth.

"Fine work. Splendid!" Nodding in delight, the general set off at a walk.

As he watched the general go, the cavalryman, still holding his bloodstained sword, took up his place behind the other Chinese. Judging by his attitude, he appeared to be enjoying the slaughter even more than the general. Taking a seat on the willow stump, Taguchi pondered the scene. Once again, the cavalryman raised his sword aloft. But the whiskered Chinese, silent, neck outstretched, didn't so much as bat an eyelid.

Sitting in his saddle, one of the officers accompanying the general, Lieutenant Colonel Hozumi, surveyed the cold spring plain. But his eyes saw neither the leafless thicket in the distance nor the stone tablet that lay fallen by the roadside; for in his head rang the words of his once beloved Stendhal:

Whenever I see a man decked in medals, I cannot help thinking how many cruelties he must have committed in order to be given such reward . . .

Recollecting himself, the lieutenant colonel realized that he was lagging far behind the general. With a slight shudder, he urged his mount on. His gold aiguillettes glittered in the pale sunlight shining down around them.

3. CAMP THEATRICALS

On the afternoon of 4th May 1905, in the thirty-eighth year of Meiji, the Headquarters of the ——th Army stationed at Ajiniupu, having conducted that morning a memorial service for the dead, was planning some entertainment. It was to be performed in one of those open-air theatres so often found in Chinese villages. Efforts at staging went as far as hanging a curtain in front of a hastily improvised set, but crowds of soldiers had nevertheless gathered, well before the appointed hour, on the straw matting. To call this mob clad in drab khaki, their bayonets by their sides, an "audience" would doubtless be to invite mockery. Yet the cheery smiles brightening their faces made the scene all the more touching.

Officers from Headquarters, led by the general, along with others from the Inspectorate of Logistics and foreign military attachés, took their seats in a slightly raised row at the back. The glitter of the offic-ers' epaulettes and the adjutants' sashes was a far cry from the rank-and-file of the audience. One foreign attaché in particular, a notorious fool, contributed especially to this display of splendour, outshining even the general.

That day the general was in high spirits. As he made conversation with one of his adjutants, he perused the programme—and all the while, like a ray of sunlight, an amiable smile floated in his eyes.

At last the appointed hour had arrived. From behind the skilfully painted curtain, decorated as it was with a rising sun and a motif of cherry blossoms, the wooden clappers rang out deafeningly. Then, in one smooth, swift motion, a hand belonging to the second lieutenant who was in charge of the entertain-ment drew back the curtain.

The set showed a Japanese room. That it was a grain merchant's shop was only hinted at by bags of rice stacked in a corner. Clad in an apron, the merchant entered, clapping his hands together and shouting, "O-Nabeya, O-Nabeya!" The maidservant, taller than her master, her hair done in the traditional "gingko leaf" style, appeared at the summons. Thereupon a one-act impromptu scene began, the plot of which merits no retelling.

Whenever something farcical took place on stage, laughter arose from the audience seated on the straw matting. Even the officers seated behind were mostly laughing. The farce, however, became all the more absurd, as if the players were trying to compete with the audience's laughter, until at last the merchant, now wearing only a loincloth, began to wrestle with the maidservant, now clad in nothing but a red slip.

The laughter grew louder. One captain from the inspectorate was even on the verge of applauding, when an infuriated, seething voice suddenly lashed out over the eddying laughter like the crack of a whip.

"This is a disgrace! The curtain! Draw the curtain!"

The voice belonged to the general. Resting both gloved hands on the hilt of his broad sabre, he was glaring sternly at the stage. As ordered, the second lieutenant hastily drew the curtain in the face of the dumbfounded players. The audience on the mats froze; but for the faint murmuring of voices, everything faded into silence.

The foreign attachés and Lieutenant Colonel Hozumi, who was sitting beside them, thought the silence a great pity. Naturally, the farce had not raised a smile on the lieutenant colonel's face, but he was broad-minded enough at least to sympathise with the soldiers' enjoyment. Moreover, having spent several years studying in Europe, he knew foreigners too well to worry himself about whether it was right and proper to let them see naked wrestling.

"Whatever's the matter?" the French attaché asked in astonishment, turning to the lieutenant colonel.

"The general ordered that the performance be stopped."

"But why?"

"Because it's obscene. The general abhors obscenity."

As he spoke, the clappers sounded once again from the stage. The soldiers, who had been sitting in total silence, began to perk up at the noise; here and there, applause rang out. Relieved, Lieutenant Colonel Hozumi looked around. All of the officers sitting alongside him seemed somewhat ill at ease, glancing fleetingly at the stage and then away again; among them only one, his hands resting on his sabre, had his eyes fixed on the stage where the curtain had been drawn back.

The next piece, in contrast to the preceding one, was a classical romance. On the stage there was only a folding screen and a lighted oil lamp. A mature woman with high cheekbones was drinking sake with a bull-necked townsman. From time to time, in a shrill voice, the woman addressed her companion as "young master" . . . But Lieutenant Colonel Hozumi was no longer watching the stage—for he had been transported by memory. He saw a boy of around twelve leaning against a handrail in the gallery of the Ryūsei-za. On the stage were strung up branches of cherry blossoms, and the backdrop showed a town with many lights. Spellbound, scarcely daring to breathe, the boy gazed down at the stage, watching the samurai Fuwa Banzaemon—then played by Wakō, popularly known as "the tuppenny Danjūrō"—strike poses as he held his broad straw hat. Yes, he too had known a time like that in his life . . .

"Stop the performance! Draw the curtain! The curtain!"

Like a bomb exploding, the general's voice shattered the lieutenant colonel's reveries. Returning his gaze to the stage, he saw the flustered ensign already running across with the curtain. In that time, however, he managed to spot two obi—a man's and a woman's—hanging over the top of a folding screen.

The lieutenant colonel's lips creased into a wry smile.

"How wildly tactless of the officer in charge of all this. If the general won't allow them to show a man and woman wrestling, then he's hardly likely to sit idly by and watch a love scene." Contemplating this, the lieutenant colonel looked over to the seat from where the angry words had issued: the general, in his distemper, was still reprimanding the officer responsible.

Suddenly, the lieutenant colonel overheard a sharp-tongued American officer remark to the French attaché sitting beside him:

"General N—— doesn't have it too easy, what with being commander of the army and the chief censor . . ."

Ten minutes later and the third play finally began. This time, the soldiers didn't even bother to applaud when the clappers sounded.

Lieutenant Colonel Hozumi pityingly surveyed the khaki-clad troops, none of whom dared speak aloud. "Poor things. They can't even watch a play without having someone look over their shoulders."

The set of the third play was composed of a black backdrop and a couple of willows standing on the stage. Where exactly these willows had been procured was anybody's guess, but they were the genuine article, and their leaves a vivid shade of green. A man with whiskers, apparently a police inspector, was hectoring a young constable. Hozumi glanced down dubiously at his programme, on which was written:

The Pistol Bandit Shimizu Sadakichi
Scene: His arrest at the riverbank

After the inspector had made his exit, the young constable, gazing heavenward in an exaggerated manner, delivered a drawn-out lamentation. The gist of it was that he had been on the pistol bandit's trail for quite some time but had never succeeded in apprehending him. Then—was it a shadow he saw? He decided to conceal himself in the river, so that his adversary should not see him. He vanished, crawling headfirst through the black backdrop. Even to the eyes of the favourably disposed audience, it looked more like climbing into a mosquito net than wading into water. For a while, all that filled the empty stage was the sound of the big drum, calling to mind the lapping of waves. Then suddenly, a blind man appeared on stage. Tapping his stick in front of him, he was about to advance when the constable burst through the black curtain. "Pistol Bandit Shimizu Sadakichi, you're under arrest!" he shouted, lunging at the blind man. The latter immediately took up a defensive stance. His eyes opened wide.

"It's a pity his eyes are too small," the lieutenant colonel thought, smiling to himself at this puerile criticism.

A tussle broke out on stage. True to his sobriquet, the bandit produced a pistol. Twice, thrice, in rapid succession, the pistol spat fire. Yet the constable ultimately succeeded in tying a rope around the faux-blind man. The audience was abuzz, but still not a word was spoken.

The lieutenant colonel glanced at the general. As before, the latter was keenly observing the action on stage, but this time the expression on his face was far gentler.

The inspector and his assistant came running onto the stage from the opposite side, but the constable, wounded by a bullet during the fight with the bandit, had already collapsed, unconscious. The inspector revived him, while his assistant deftly caught the end of the rope binding the bandit. A pathetic scene, fashioned in the old style, ensued between the inspector and the constable. Like a fabled magistrate of a past era, the inspector asked the constable whether he had any last words. The constable said that his mother still lived in his hometown. The inspector told him not to worry about his mother. Was there nothing else he wished to say before he breathed his last? There was nothing. He had caught the pistol bandit, and with that his life's wish had been fulfilled.

Just then, amid the hush of the auditorium, the general's voice rang out a third time. On this occasion, however, the voice was not chastening but filled with deep emotion:

"Now, there's a fine fellow! A true son of Japan!"

Once again Hozumi looked askance at the general. Traces of tears glistened on the general's sunburnt cheeks. "He's a good man, the general," thought Hozumi with slight disdain and, at the same time, a degree of affection.

To the thunder of applause, the curtain was drawn slowly across the stage. Seizing the opportunity, Lieutenant Colonel Hozumi rose from his chair and left the auditorium.

Half an hour later, with a cigarette in his mouth, the lieutenant colonel found himself walking with a fellow-soldier, Major Nakamura, in the wastelands on the outskirts of the village.

"The play was a great success. His Excellency seemed to enjoy it," said Major Nakamura as he twirled the tips of his Kaiser moustache.

"The play? Oh, that pistol bandit?"

"Not just the pistol bandit. His Excellency summoned the officer in charge of the entertainment and ordered him to put on an extra scene. Something about Genzō Akagaki. What *was* it called? Perhaps it was *Tokuri no hanare*—the parting before the bottle."

Smiling with his eyes, Lieutenant Colonel Hozumi surveyed the expanse of fields. A gossamer haze was drifting over a landscape in which the kaoliangs had already turned green.

"That, too, was a great success," Major Nakamura continued.

"I hear that His Excellency has ordered the officer in charge to put on some entertainment this evening at seven o'clock."

"Entertainment, you say? What kind? Story-telling?"

"You must be joking. *The Travels of Kōmon Mito* . . ."

Lieutenant Colonel Hozumi smiled wryly, but his companion continued blithely and obliviously:

"Apparently His Excellency is fond of Kōmon Mito. 'As a faithful subject,' he said, 'I esteem Kōmon Mito and Kiyomasa Katō most of all.'"

Without replying, Lieutenant Colonel Hozumi looked up at the sky overhead. Through the willow branches, he could see clouds of mica being blown across the sky. Hozumi sighed.

"It's spring. Even in Manchuria."

"Back home, they'll still be wearing lined kimonos." The major thought of Tokyo. He thought of his wife, who was a fine cook. He thought of his children at school. Then he was overcome by a vague feeling of melancholy.

"Look, the apricots are in bloom," Lieutenant Colonel Hozumi said, pointing wistfully to a cluster of vermilion-coloured blossom hanging over a distant mud wall. *Écoute-moi, Madeleine* . . . Hugo's lines drifted unexpectedly into his mind.

4. FATHER AND SON

An evening in October 1918, in the seventh year of Taishō. Major General Nakamura, who had at one time been that very same major stationed at Army Headquarters, was reclining idly in an armchair in his Western-style drawing room, smoking a Havana cigar. The passing of a leisurely score of years had made of Nakamura a charming old gentleman. Tonight in particular—perhaps it was the kimono that did it—there was something gentler and kinder than usual about his balding forehead and the fleshy folds around his mouth. As he leant back in the chair, he took in his surroundings slowly and sighed all of a sudden.

Wherever one looked, the walls were adorned with framed photogravures, all reproductions of European paintings. One of them depicted a melancholy girl leaning against a window. Another showed a landscape: cypresses backlit by the sun. In the harsh electric light, these pictures lent a curiously austere, rather chill air to the old-fashioned drawing room. For some reason, the major general did not find the atmosphere to his liking.

The silence lingered for some time, before it was broken by a light knock on the door.

"Come in."

At these words, the tall figure of a young man in university uniform entered the room. The youth stood in front of the major general and, resting his hand on a chair, asked brusquely:

"Is there something you wanted, Father?"

"There is. Sit down."

The youth sat down obediently. "What is it?"

The major general looked dubiously at the gold buttons on the youth's chest.

"Where were you today?"

"There was a memorial service for Kawai. You wouldn't know him, Father—he was a fellow student in the literary faculty. I've only just returned."

The major general gave a slight nod and exhaled a thick cloud of cigar smoke. Wearily, he brought himself to speak of this urgent business.

"Was it you who swapped the pictures on the wall?"

"Yes, I hadn't had the chance to tell you. I rearranged them this morning. Shouldn't I have?"

"No, it was the right thing to do. All the same, I think I should have liked to keep the portrait of His Excellency General N——."

"Here?" The youth smiled involuntarily.

"Is there something so wrong with that?"

"Nothing wrong per se, but . . . but wouldn't it be a little odd?"

"There are other portraits here, aren't there?" The major general indicated the chimney breast. On the wall, from his frame, a fifty-year-old Rembrandt gazed serenely down at the major general.

"That's hardly the same thing. You can't hang General N—— next to that."

"I can't? Well, there's nothing to be done about it then," said Nakamura, acquiescing. But as he exhaled another cloud of cigar smoke, he continued calmly: "What do you . . . or rather, what do your peers think of His Excellency?"

"We don't think anything in particular. He was a great soldier, I suppose."

The youth noticed in his aged father's eyes a trace of his evening cup of sake.

"Yes, he was a great soldier, but in fact His Excellency was also a man of many virtues and great kindness."

Almost sentimentally, Nakamura began to tell an anecdote about the general. The episode had occurred in the years after the Russo-Japanese War, on a visit that Nakamura paid the general at his villa in Nasuno. As he was arriving at the villa, Nakamura was informed by an officer on duty that the general and his wife had just gone out for a walk in the mountains. Knowing the way, Nakamura immediately set off in pursuit of them. After two or three hundred yards, he spotted the general in his heavy cotton kimono, standing beside his wife. Nakamura stopped and spoke to the old couple for a short while, but the general showed no signs of moving. "Might I ask whether you have any business here?" he enquired. The general burst out laughing. "The fact is, my wife has just told me she wishes to relieve herself, so the schoolchildren walking with us have gone to look for somewhere while we wait." It was about the same time of year—when scattered chestnuts in their burrs lay at the roadsides.

Nakamura narrowed his eyes and, with a look of satisfaction, smiled. From the forest, where the leaves had turned golden, a group of four or five rowdy schoolchildren came running. Paying no mind to Nakamura, they surrounded the couple and all at once began reporting on the places they had found for the general's wife. An innocent competition began, each child begging her to go with him. "Well, you had better draw lots," said the general, turning once again to Nakamura with a smile . . .

"A tale of innocence. But we couldn't tell it to a Westerner, could we?" The youth couldn't help laughing.

"He had a way about him. That's why boys of twelve or thirteen would think of His Excellency as an uncle figure. The general was not at all, as you seem to think, a mere soldier."

His story now over, Nakamura again looked at the Rembrandt above the fireplace. "Was he, too, a man of character?"

"He was a great artist, Father."

"Yes, but how does he compare to General N——?"

A flush of bewilderment crossed the youth's face. "It's hard to say . . . he's closer to us in spirit than His Excellency."

"And is the general so very distant?"

"How shall I put it? . . . Take Kawai, for example, whose memorial I attended today. Like the general, Kawai also committed suicide, but before he did . . ."—here the youth looked earnestly at his father's face—"he didn't see fit to have his photograph taken."

Now a look of bewilderment flashed in the major general's kind eyes.

"But shouldn't one have one's photograph taken? After all, it's one last act of commemoration, and . . ."

"But who's it for?"

"It isn't *for* anyone. But don't we wish to see the face of His Excellency in his final moments?"

"I doubt at least that General N—— would have seen it that way. I can understand to some degree the general's wish to commit suicide, but what I cannot fathom is why he should have his photograph taken. I daresay it wasn't to be displayed in some shop window afterwards . . ."

"That's a very harsh view of it," Nakamura interrupted the youth indignantly. "His Excellency wasn't so vulgar. He was a man of sincerity through and through."

The youth's voice and face, however, retained their composure.

"I don't doubt he wasn't vulgar. And I can well imagine that he was a man of sincerity. But all the same, that sincerity is rather difficult to comprehend nowadays. Nor do I believe that it'll be any clearer to those who come after us."

A disagreeable silence ensued between father and son.

"Times are different, aren't they?" said the major general at last.

"Yes, well . . ." the youth began. But as he listened to what was going on outside the window, his eyes took on a distant expression.

"It's raining, Father."

"Raining?" Nakamura stretched out his legs, only too glad to change the subject. "We'll be lucky if the quinces don't fall again . . ."

MADONNA IN BLACK

From the depths of the vale of tears, from the depths of the vale of sorrow, we call to you with our prayer . . . O merciful, most holy Mother of God, most gentle Queen of Heaven, O Sancta Maria!

(From a Japanese translation of the "Ave Maria")

"WHAT DO YOU MAKE of it, then?"

With these words Tashiro placed the statuette of Maria-Kannon on the table.

Maria-Kannon . . . Thus are called the figurines of the Virgin Mary, ordinarily made of white porcelain, to which Christians prayed so often during the years when the Catholic faith was forbidden in Japan. But the statuette that Tashiro had shown me was unlike those seen in museums and any run-of-the-mill private collections. For one, the foot-tall statuette, with the exception of the face, had been carved entirely from ebony. Moreover, the necklace of crosses hanging about the neck was inlayed with gold and mother-of-pearl—a work of the most exquisite craftsmanship. Lastly, there was the face, so beautifully fashioned from ivory, with lips a fleck of coral-like vermilion.

I folded my arms and silently beheld the beautiful face of this "Madonna in Black". As I gazed at it, however, a strange expression seemed to flit across its ivory countenance. But "strange" is too weak a word. No, I had the distinct impression that a cruel smile tinged with malice pervaded its every feature.

"Well, what do you make of it?" Tashiro repeated, smiling proudly, as any collector would, and glancing now at me, now at Maria-Kannon standing on the table.

"It's certainly a rarity. But don't you think there's something uncanny about the face?"

"Yes, you wouldn't exactly call those features benevolent-looking, would you? In point of fact, this statuette comes with a rather strange history."

"Strange, you say?"

Instinctively I shifted my gaze from the statuette to Tashiro. His face wore an unexpectedly sober expression. He raised the statuette from the table, but immediately set it down again in its former place.

"Yes, it's said that this Madonna bodes ill. Instead of warding off evil, she brings misfortune."

"I don't believe it."

"Be that as it may, it's what they say. In fact, they say that something of the kind happened to its former owner."

As he lowered himself into a chair with a pensive, melancholy look in his eyes, Tashiro bade me take a seat in the chair opposite him. As I sat down, I asked with an involuntary note of suspicion in my voice: "Can it really be true?"

Tashiro, who had graduated from the university a year or two ahead of me, had the formidable reputation of a talented legal mind and, insofar as I knew, was well educated, modern-thinking, and placed very little faith in so-called supernatural phenomena. Thus, for Tashiro to bring up something in this vein, it was hardly likely that this "strange history" would be some absurd tale of the unexpected.

As I repeated my question, Tashiro struck a match and slowly brought the flame to his pipe.

"Judge for yourself. At any rate, there's something sinister about this Maria-Kannon. I'll be only too glad to tell you the story, if you care to hear it . . ."

*

Before this Maria-Kannon came into my possession, it belonged to the wealthy Inami family, who lived in a certain village in Niigata Prefecture. Of course, the antique was not regarded as such, but rather as a deity to which the family prayed for its prosperity.

The head of the family, old Inami, and I read law together at the university. He has quite a number of commercial interests and a hand in the running of a certain bank—in a word, he's a real man of business. It was in connection with those interests that I even had occasion to be of service to him once or twice. I rather suspect that it was a token of his gratitude. In any case, when Inami came up to Tokyo one year, he brought me this Maria-Kannon, which had been in his family for generations.

It was from Inami that I then heard this so-called "strange history", but of course he himself didn't believe a word of the legend. All the same, he gave me a potted account of the Madonna's history, just as he himself had heard it from his mother.

Seemingly it happened in the autumn when Inami's mother, O-Ei, turned either ten or eleven. So, it must have been in the closing years of the Kaei era, when Commodore Perry's Black Ships were stalking the harbour at Uraga. That autumn, O-Ei's brother, the eight-year-old Mosaku, took ill with a severe bout of measles. After the death of their parents from disease a couple of years earlier, O-Ei and her brother had been left in the care of their grandmother, who was then already in her seventh decade. It isn't difficult to imagine how Mosaku's illness worried this elderly woman, Inami's great-grandmother. No matter what the doctors tried, Mosaku's illness only worsened; within a week, talk turned to his impending death.

Then, one night, the grandmother crept into the room where O-Ei was sound asleep. Having woken the sleeping girl and forced her out of bed, she helped the girl, with great fuss and without a maid, to dress properly. O-Ei had the vague feeling that she was still dreaming, but the grandmother took her by the hand and, lighting the desolate hallway with a dim paper lantern, hauled the girl into the storehouse, which was rarely visited even by day.

In the depths of the storehouse there stood an old white wooden shrine dedicated to the goddess Inari, to guard against fires. The grandmother extracted a key that was tucked into her *obi* and opened the door to the shrine. There, bathed in the lantern's dim light, standing behind the ancient-looking brocade of the shrine's curtain, was this very Maria-Kannon. As soon as O-Ei saw it, fear overcame her; amid the perfect silence of the storehouse in the dead of night, she instinctively clung to her grandmother's knees and began to sob. However, the grandmother, who was usually so kind and affectionate, paid no heed to O-Ei's tears and, sitting before the shrine to Maria-Kannon, reverently made the sign of the cross before offering up a prayer that was incomprehensible to O-Ei.

After about ten minutes of this, the old woman calmly lifted up O-Ei and, comforting the frightened girl, sat her down beside her. Thereupon she began to pray to the ebony statuette in a way that O-Ei could understand.

"Blessed Virgin Mary, all that I have in this world is my eight-year-old grandson Mosaku and his sister O-Ei, whom I have brought to you. As you can see, she is still too young to take a husband, so if anything were to happen to Mosaku now, the Inami House would be robbed of its heir. Oh, please, do not let such misfortune befall us! Save Mosaku's life! If it is too much to ask that you hear the prayer of a wretched soul like me, then at least spare him for as long as I still draw breath. I am old and shall hardly live long; soon I shall give up my soul unto Him. But by then, God willing, my granddaughter O-Ei will have come of age. I beg of you, let your mercy be upon us, remove the Angel of Death's sword that threatens to strike at Mosaku's body, at least until I close my eyes for all eternity."

Thus the old woman prayed fervently, bowing her head with its short-cut hair. Then, when the prayer was finished and the little girl timidly lifted her head, she could see—or was it her imagination?—Maria-Kannon smiling. Naturally, O-Ei cried out in her little voice and once again clung to her grandmother's knees. But the old woman wore a look of satisfaction and, as she stroked her granddaughter's back, repeated several times:

"Come, we can go now . . . Our Lady has deigned to hear Obāsan's prayer . . ."

And so, on the following day, as though the old woman's prayer had indeed been heard, Mosaku's fever broke, and if the previous day he had been in a state of delirium, then today he was gradually coming to his senses. It is difficult to describe the grandmother's joy as she looked on. Inami's mother told him that she could never forget her grandmother's face, laughing and crying at one and the same time. Having made sure that the boy was peacefully asleep, the old woman decided to rest a little after several nights spent keeping watch by his bed. She ordered a bed to be made up in the adjoining room and lay down there, although usually she slept in her own room.

O-Ei sat by the old woman's pillow, playing tiddly-winks. She said that her grandmother had used up every last ounce of her strength and immediately fell into a deep sleep, as though she were dead. Around an hour passed in this way, until an elderly maid, who had been checking on Mosaku, softly opened the sliding door separating the two rooms. With a note of panic in her voice, she asked:

"Miss, you couldn't wake the mistress, could you?"

O-Ei rushed to the old woman's side and tugged on the sleeve of her nightgown, calling: "Obāsan, Obāsan!"

But the strangest of things: no matter how much O-Ei called her, the old woman, who usually slept so lightly, just wouldn't respond. Meanwhile, with a look of disbelief, the maid came over, but as soon as she saw the old woman's face, like one possessed, she suddenly started tugging at the kimono and with tears of desperation began to cry out: "Mistress! Mistress!" However, the old woman didn't so much as stir, while pale lilac shadows had now fallen around her eyes. Presently another maid threw open the door in a fluster and, her face pale with terror, called out in a trembling voice:

"Mistress! It's the young master . . . Mistress!"

Of course, it was clear to O-Ei from these words that Mosaku's condition had taken a sharp turn for the worse. But still the old woman just lay there motionless, her eyes tightly shut, as though she couldn't hear the maid who had broken down in tears beside her pillow . . .

Not even ten minutes later, Mosaku also breathed his last. According to her promise, Maria-Kannon had killed him only after the old woman was dead.

*

Having finished his story, Tashiro lifted his melancholy eyes, which came to rest on my face.

"So, what do you make of it?" he asked. "Surely you can't think that it really happened?"

I hesitated.

"Well . . . No, but . . . It's difficult to say."

For a moment Tashiro was silent. Then, striking another match and relighting his pipe, he said:

"I think it did happen. The real question is whether or not this Madonna is to blame. Come to think of it, you haven't read the inscription on the base, have you? Take a look. Do you see the engraving? *Desine fata deum flecti sperare precando* . . . 'Cease to hope that the decrees of Heaven can bend to prayer.'"

With an instinctive sense of fear, I beheld the Madonna—the very embodiment of fate. Clad in blackest ebony, she wore a look of eternal indifference, her beautiful ivory face crossed by a cruel smile tinged with malice.

COGWHEELS

I. RAINCOATS

I WAS ON MY way to Tokyo to attend the wedding reception of an acquaintance. In a taxi, satchel in hand, I was racing to a station on the Tōkaidō line from my home in a seaside resort. Dense, almost unbroken rows of pine trees lined both sides of the road and, as we swept along, I pondered the vanishing likelihood of my making the train in time. I was sharing the taxi with the owner of a barbershop. He was cylindrically plump, like a *natsume*, and sported a short beard. Even as I worried about the time, I still managed to exchange the occasional word with him.

"Strange things do happen, do they not?" he observed. "I hear there have been sightings of a ghost up at Mr ——'s villa. Even in the middle of the day, they say."

"In the middle of the day, eh?" I replied distractedly, my eyes drawn by a view of distant pine-covered
hills basking in the light of the westering winter sun.

"Not on days when the weather's fine, though.
Mostly when it rains."

"It might catch its death in weather like that."

"Very droll . . . Though they do say that it wears a
raincoat."

With a cry of its horn, the taxi pulled up outside
the station. I took my leave of the barber and rushed
inside, but, just as I'd feared, the train for Tokyo had
pulled out a couple of minutes earlier. Sitting alone on
a bench in the waiting room, staring vacantly out of
the window, was a man in a raincoat. Remembering
the story I had only just heard about the ghost, I
grinned and, thinking no more of it, resigned myself
to waiting for the next train in the café opposite the
station.

Actually, "café" is much too grand a term for what
this place was. I sat down at a corner table and ordered
a cup of cocoa. The oilcloth covering the table was a
rustic blue gingham, but its edges were worn and
revealed a drab, dirty-looking canvas beneath.

The cocoa tasted of animal glue. As I sipped it, I
looked around at the deserted room. Slips of paper
affixed to dust-coated walls announced the fare on

offer: "*Oyako-donburi*", "Cutlets", "Omelette made with local eggs". These paper slips seemed so typical of the countryside around the Tōkaidō line—the countryside, where electric-powered locomotives passed between fields of barley and cabbage.

By the time I boarded the next train for Tokyo, the sun was beginning to set. I always travelled second class, but this time, for some reason, I took third.

In the already crowded carriage, I was surrounded by a bevy of schoolgirls on their way back from a trip to Ōiso or some such place. I lit a cigarette and observed as they chatted away incessantly, all in high spirits.

"Mr Cameraman, what does *love scene* mean?" asked a girl of around fourteen, using the English term.

Sitting opposite me, this "Mr Cameraman", who had seemingly accompanied them on the excursion, was doing his level best to avoid giving a straight answer. But still the girl kept on plying him with all manner of questions. When it suddenly occurred to me that her grating intonations could be caused by a nasal infection, I couldn't help but smile. The girl beside me, who must have been twelve or thirteen, then went over to sit on the young schoolmistress' lap, slipping her arm around the woman's neck and stroking her cheek with her other hand. Between talking to her friends, she would tell the teacher:

"Miss, you're so pretty! You have such pretty eyes!"

To me they seemed so much more like women than schoolgirls—that is, if you ignored the way they munched on unpeeled apples and unwrapped their caramels. The one I took to be the eldest happened to step on someone's toe as she passed by me. "Oh, I am sorry!" she exclaimed. Curiously, it was her very maturity that made her seem more like a schoolgirl than the rest. The cigarette still hanging between my lips, I couldn't suppress a scornful laugh as I pondered the contradiction of my own impressions.

The electric lights in the train had been illuminated by the time we finally pulled into one of the suburban stations. A cold wind was blowing as I stepped down onto the platform. I crossed the footbridge to wait for the connecting train, when quite by chance I bumped into T——, an acquaintance who worked for a certain well-known firm. As we waited, we discussed this and that, including the current recession. T—— was, of course, much better informed on such matters than I. Yet, despite the hard economic times, on one of his powerful fingers was a splendid turquoise ring.

"That's quite some ring you're wearing."

"This? A friend who went over to Harbin persuaded me to buy it from him. He's in quite a bind now that he can't do business with the cooperatives."

Fortunately, the train that arrived was not as crowded as the previous one. We sat down next to one another and continued talking. T—— had just returned to Tokyo that spring from a posting in Paris, and so it was Paris that dominated our conversation. We talked about Madame Caillaux, about crab cuisine, and about the royal prince who was on an overseas tour.

"The situation in France isn't as bad as people think it is. It's just that the French are stubbornly opposed to paying taxes, and so their governments go on falling."

"But the franc has plummeted."

"That's if you believe what you read in the newspapers. Over there the papers will tell you that Japan has nothing but flooding and earthquakes."

Just then, a man in a raincoat came and sat down opposite us. This gave me a rather eerie feeling, and I felt an urge to tell T—— about the ghost story I had heard. But before I could, T—— tipped the handle of his cane to the left and, still facing forward, said to me in a hushed tone: "Do you see that woman over there? The one in the dark-grey woollen shawl?"

"With the Western hairstyle?"

"Yes, the one carrying something wrapped in a *furoshiki* under her arm. She was in Karuizawa this summer—always wearing chic European clothes."

To see her now, however, anyone would have thought her quite shabby-looking. While I spoke with T——, I stole a few glances at her. Her face betrayed a hint of madness between the brows. Moreover, poking out of the *furoshiki* was a sea sponge with a leopard's spots.

"When I saw her at Karuizawa, she was always dancing with some young American. Bright young things . . . Isn't that what they say?"

As I said goodbye to T——, I realized that the man in the raincoat had already vanished. Satchel in hand, I made my way from the station to a hotel. Tall buildings lined both sides of the street. As I was walking, I suddenly recalled the pine forest. I also became aware that something strange had entered my field of vision—a set of steadily spinning transparent cogwheels. It was not the first time that I had experienced this. It was always the same: the number of cogwheels would gradually increase until they blocked half my field of vision. It would not last for long, however, and after a few moments they would vanish, only to be replaced by the onset of a headache. My eye doctor kept telling me to cut down on smoking so as to rid myself of these optical illusions (if that is indeed what they were), but I had started seeing these cogwheels before I turned twenty, well before I took up smoking. "Here we go again," I thought to myself, covering my right eye to test the vision in the left one. As expected, there was nothing wrong with the left eye, but behind the lid of the right several cogwheels were spinning. I quickened my pace as the buildings on my right gradually vanished.

The cogwheels had already disappeared by the time I entered the hotel lobby, but I was left with a headache. As I was checking my hat and overcoat, I decided to reserve a room. I then telephoned a magazine publisher to discuss money.

I could see that the wedding banquet was well underway. I found myself a seat at the far corner of the table and began moving my knife and fork. There must have been fifty-odd people seated at the horseshoe-shaped table, and all of them, from the bride and groom at the centre down, were naturally in high spirits. For my part, however, under the glare of the electric lights, I sank ever deeper into a depression. In the hope of escaping this feeling, I struck up a conversation with my neighbour, an old gentleman sporting a white beard every bit like a lion's mane. I knew him to be a renowned scholar of the Chinese classics, to which topic our conversation soon turned.

"When all's said and done, the *qilin* is really a kind of unicorn," I ventured. "And the *fenghuang* is what in the West they call a phoenix . . ."

The renowned scholar seemed to take an interest in these remarks, but the longer I continued the mechanical process of making conversation, the more I began to feel the onset of a pathologically destructive urge. Not only did I declare that the legendary emperors Yao and Shun were "obviously" fictional creations, but I even claimed that the author of the *Spring and Autumn Annals* was of the much later Han period. At this, the scholar's face assumed an expression of undisguised displeasure. Turning away, he cut me off with an almost tiger-like growl:

"If you say that Yao and Shun never existed, you make a liar of Confucius. And it is unimaginable that the great sage would lie."

I offered no rejoinder, of course, and applied my cutlery to the slice of meat resting on my plate. As I did, I spotted a tiny maggot silently squirming at the edge of the meat. The sight of it called to mind the English word *worm*, which I decided must stand for another legendary creature like the *qilin* and the *fenghuang.* I laid down my knife and fork and watched my champagne glass being filled.

When the banquet was finally over, I walked down a deserted corridor to shut myself away in the room I had taken. The corridor struck me as more like that of a prison than a hotel. Fortunately, however, my head-ache had at last subsided.

My bag, along with my hat and overcoat, had been brought to the room. The overcoat hanging on the wall looked like my own silhouette. I hastily flung it into a wardrobe in the corner of the room. I then went over to the dresser and stared at my reflection in the mirror. In the face staring back at me, I could see the bones protruding from under the skin. With total clar-ity, the image of the maggot suddenly surfaced in my memory.

I opened the door, stepped out into the corridor, and set off aimlessly. At the far end, where the corridor turned, leading down towards the lobby, stood a tall standard lamp with a green shade, its light reflected brilliantly in a glass door. The sight of it imparted to me a feeling of tranquillity. I sat down in a nearby chair and pondered various things, but not even five minutes had gone by when my thoughts were interrupted: another raincoat—this time lying draped over the back of an adjacent sofa, where someone had tossed it.

"But why a raincoat in this cold weather?" I wondered.

Thinking this, I retraced my steps along the corridor. At the porters' station there was no one to be seen, although I could just about make out some voices. In response to something, one was saying in English, "All right." All right? I struggled to grasp the precise meaning of the exchange. *All right? All right?* What in the world could be all right?

In my room, of course, there could be only stillness, yet for some reason I had a strange premonition as I opened the door, about to enter. After some hesitation, I steeled myself to go in. Taking care not to look at myself in the mirror, I sat down at the desk in an easy chair upholstered in green morocco leather, like a lizard's skin. I opened my satchel, took out some writing paper, and attempted to work on a story I had been writing. But the pen, even after I dipped it in ink, refused to move. And when at last it did, it just kept writing the same words over and over: "All right . . . All right . . . All right, sir . . . All right . . ."

Suddenly the telephone by the bed rang. Startled, I stood up and held the receiver to my ear.

"Who is it?" I asked.

"It's me. *Me* . . ." It was my niece.

"What is it? Has something happened?"

"Yes, something terrible," she said. "You see, there's been a terrible accident, I called Auntie's house and she—"

"An accident?"

"Yes. You must come quickly. Right away."

The line went dead. I replaced the receiver and automatically pressed the button to summon a porter. I was conscious that my hand was trembling. No one came in response to the bell. More out of distress than impatience, I kept pressing and pressing the button. But at last I understood what Fate had been trying to tell me with those words: "All right."

That afternoon, in the countryside not far from Tokyo, my elder sister's husband had thrown himself under a train. Despite the cold weather, he had been wearing a raincoat.

I am in that same hotel room even now, still writing that same story. Nobody passes along the corridor at night, but sometimes I can hear the sound of wings outside my door. Perhaps someone is keeping birds nearby.

2. VENGEANCE

I woke in the hotel room around eight o'clock in the morning. Strangely, however, when I tried to get out of bed, I found only one slipper. Over the past year or so, this particular phenomenon had been causing me no end of fear and anxiety, reminding me as it did of the one-sandalled prince of Greek myth. I rang for the porter and had him look for the slipper's pair. Wearing a puzzled look, he searched the small room.

"Here it is," he said. "It was in the bathroom."

"I wonder how it ended up there . . ."

"Rats, maybe."

After the porter left, I drank some black coffee and set to finishing off my story. The square window, framed with volcanic stone, gave onto a snow-covered garden. Each time I set down my pen, my gaze would lose itself in the snow, which, spread out beneath a budding winter daphne, was befouled by the soot and smoke of the city. The view pained my heart. As I sat there smoking, my pen again motionless, I thought about all manner of things—about my wife, my children, above all my sister's husband . . .

Before committing suicide, my brother-in-law had been suspected of arson. And little wonder: he had insured the house for twice its value just before it burned down. As if that were not enough, he was also serving a suspended sentence for perjury. What disturbed me even more than his suicide, however, was that whenever I returned to Tokyo, I was sure to see a fire of some sort. Once it was a farmer burning his hillside fields that I spotted from a train window; another time it was a fire in the Tokiwabashi neighbourhood that I saw from a taxi (together with my wife and children). Thus, even before his house went up in flames, it was only natural that I should have had a premonition of the fire.

"Maybe our house will burn down this year," I said to my wife.

"You mustn't say things like that . . . It's bad luck. Still, it would be terrible if we did have a fire. Our insurance is so paltry . . ."

It was not the first time that we had that conversation. Still, my house had been spared, so far . . . I tried to brush aside these delusions and once again take up my pen, but writing even a single line was beyond me. I finally gave up and stretched out on the bed to read Tolstoy's "Polikoushka". The protagonist of the story was a complex muddle of vanity, morbidity and ambition. Yet, with but a few minor alterations, the tragi-comedy of his life could have been a caricature of mine. More and more I was gripped by an eerie feeling, sensing in the protagonist's tragicomedy the cold smile of Fate. Not even an hour had passed when I leapt out of bed and, with all my might, hurled the book against the curtains in the corner of the room.

"Damn it all!"

That very moment, a large rat darted out from under the curtain and scurried diagonally across the floor into the bathroom. I bounded over to the bathroom, flung open the door to search for the rat, but there was no sign of it, even behind the white bathtub. Suddenly overcome by that eerie feeling, I hastily swapped my slippers for shoes and ran out into the deserted corridor.

The corridor was as depressing a prison as it had been on the previous day. Hanging my head, I went up and down one staircase after another until I found myself in the hotel kitchens, whose brightness took me by surprise. I could see flames moving under the ranges lining one of the walls. As I passed through the room, I could feel the cold stares of the white-hatted chefs and, at the same time, I had the sensation of having fallen into Hell. In that instant, a prayer spontaneously rose to my lips: "O Lord, correct me, but with judgement; not in Thine anger, lest Thou bring me to nothing."

I left the hotel, hurrying to my sister's along streets reflecting the blue sky in pools of melted snow. All the leaves and branches of the park trees lining the street loomed black, and each tree had a front and a back just as we human beings do. The feeling this realization brought was closer to fear than displeasure. I recalled the souls in Dante's *Inferno* who had been turned into trees and decided instead to walk on the other side of the tram tracks, where only buildings lined the street.

Yet even there I found I couldn't walk a block unmolested.

"I'm sorry to bother you like this, in the middle of the street, but . . ." It was a young man of twenty-two or -three, wearing a uniform with gold buttons. As I stared at him in silence, I noticed a mole on the left side of his nose. He removed his cap and asked timidly: "Aren't you Mr A——?"

"I am."

"I thought so . . ."

"Is there something I can do for you?"

"No, I only wanted to meet the great man himself. I'm such an admirer of your—"

Slightly doffing my hat to him, I walked on before he could finish. "Great man": this was the worst possible epithet anyone could have bestowed on me back then. I believed that I had committed all manner of sin, but still, whenever the opportunity arose, they went on calling me a "great man". I couldn't help but feel that I was somehow being mocked. By whom though? My affirmation of materialism did not allow such mysticism. Only a few months previously, I had written in a certain little niche magazine: "I have no artistic conscience; indeed, I have no conscience whatsoever. I have only nerves."

My sister had taken refuge together with her three children in a makeshift shack in a back alley. Hung with dark-brown paper, the shack seemed almost colder inside than out. We talked of many things as we warmed our hands over the brazier. My brother-in-law, a man of robust physique, had nurtured an instinctive dislike of me for being so exceedingly slight. What's more, he had openly denounced my writing as immoral. I in turn had always treated his views with cool contempt, and never once had I had a frank and open conversation with him. Yet, in speaking with my sister, I gradually began to realize that he too had been leading a hellish existence. She tried to tell me something about how he had once actually seen a ghost in a wagon-lit, but I lit a cigarette and tried my best to keep the conversation strictly financial.

"Under the circumstances," she said, "I'll have to sell just about everything."

"Yes, I suppose you will. You should be able to get something for the typewriter."

"True . . . And there are the paintings, too."

"Speaking of which, are you going to sell the portrait of N——?" (Her husband.) "Then again, it's not exactly . . ."

As I looked at the unframed pastel portrait hanging on the wall of the shack, I sensed that this was no time for flippancy. The man had thrown himself under a train, whose wheels, they said, had turned his face into a mass of flesh, leaving only his moustache intact. As if this story in itself were not unnerving enough, the portrait was a perfect likeness of him—but for the moustache, which for some reason seemed blurred to me. I wondered whether it could be a trick of the light, and so set about examining the portrait from every angle.

"What are you doing?"

"Oh, nothing . . . It's just . . . The area around the mouth . . ."

Glancing over her shoulder, my sister remarked obliviously: "Yes, it's strange, isn't it, how the moustache looks so faded."

What I had seen was no hallucination. But if it wasn't, then . . .

I decided to leave before my sister started fussing over lunch.

"You needn't run off just yet."

"I'll be back tomorrow . . . I have to go to Aoyama today."

"Oh, you're going *there*? Are you still not feeling well?"

"All I do is take pills. The sleeping tablets alone are bad enough. Veronal, Neuronal, Trional, Numal . . ."

Half an hour later, I found myself entering a building and taking a lift to the third floor. I tried pushing open the glass door to a restaurant, but it wouldn't budge. Hanging there was a lacquered sign on which was written the word CLOSED. With mounting annoyance, I gazed through the door at an arrangement of apples and bananas on a table. I turned to go. As I was leaving, two men engaged in lively conversation, apparently company employees, were entering the building. One of them happened to brush against my shoulder, and as he did I thought I heard the other say, ". . . tempting, aren't they? . . ."

I stood outside, waiting for a taxi, but not many came my way. Those few that did come were invariably yellow. (For some reason, the yellow taxis I took were forever getting into accidents.) In the end, I was able to flag down a lucky green one and decided to take it to the psychiatric hospital near the cemetery in Aoyama.

"Tempting . . . tantalizing . . . Tantalus . . . inferno . . ."

I myself had been Tantalus, gazing at the fruit through the glass door. I stared at the driver's back, cursing Dante's vision of Hell now twice brought before my eyes. Soon enough, I began to feel that anything and everything was a lie. Politics, industry, arts, science—all this seemed to me little more than a gaily coloured enamel concealing the true horror of human life. More and more, I began to feel as though I were suffocating. I opened the taxi window, but the feeling of tightness around my heart remained.

The green taxi was now finally nearing Jingū-mae. There ought to have been a side street leading to the psychiatric hospital, but for some reason I couldn't find it today. I had the driver go back and forth along the tram tracks, but at last I gave up and got out.

Eventually I found the right street and turned to go down the muddy alley, but at some point I lost my way and found myself in front of Aoyama Funeral Hall. Not once in the ten long years since Natsume-sensei's memorial service had I darkened the gate of that building. Back then I had also been unhappy, but at least I had felt at peace. As I peered in through the gate at the gravelled courtyard, I recalled the *bashō* plants of the Sōseki Retreat. I could not help sensing that my life, too, had reached its end, and that Fate had brought me here—to this cemetery, ten years on.

After leaving the psychiatric hospital, I took a taxi back to the hotel. As I got out at the entrance to the hotel, however, I saw a man in a raincoat arguing with one of the porters. With one of the porters? No, it wasn't a porter but rather a doorman in a green uniform—the one whose job was to flag down taxis. This seemed like a bad omen, and so I immediately turned back.

The sun was already beginning to set by the time I reached the Ginza. The shops lining both sides of the street and the dizzying bustle of people only made me more depressed. I was especially troubled by the jaunty way people had of walking to and fro, as if the very existence of sin were unknown to them. I carried on northward through a mix of the day's fading brightness and the electric light of streetlamps. Along the way, my eye was caught by a bookshop piled high with magazines and the like. I went in and let my eyes roam the many shelves of books. I picked out a volume of Greek mythology to leaf through. The yellow-covered book was apparently intended for children, but the line I chanced to read sent me reeling:

"Even Zeus, the greatest of all gods, is no match for those goddesses of vengeance, the Furies . . ."

Leaving the bookshop behind, I began to pick my way through the crowds, stopping as I went. Before I knew it, I could sense the unrelenting gaze of those same Furies on my back . . .

3. NIGHT

On the second floor of the Maruzen bookshop, I found a copy of Strindberg's *Legends*. I leafed through it a couple of pages at a time. The experiences it described were not so different from my own. As if that were not enough, it also had a yellow cover. I returned the book to its shelf and plucked out another thick volume at random, yet this one too had something in store for me: in one of the illustrations, there were rows of cogwheels with human eyes and noses. (The book was a collection of drawings made by psychiatric patients, collated by a certain German editor.) In the midst of my depression, I felt the spirit of revolt rise within me and, with the abandon of a compulsive gambler, began opening book after book. Every last one of them, however, concealed a needle to prick me, whether in the text or the illustrations. Every last one? I picked up *Madame Bovary*, which I had read any number of times, and even there I discovered that I myself was but another bourgeois Monsieur Bovary . . .

As the close of day drew nearer, I seemed to be the only customer on the second floor of the bookshop. I meandered among the bookcases under the electric light, stopping in front of one labelled "Religion", where I perused a volume with a green cover. The table of contents listed one of the chapters as "The Four Most Terrible Adversaries: Doubt, Fear, Arrogance, Lust". No sooner had I read those words than the spirit of revolt grew stronger in me. For me, at least, these so-called adversaries were synonymous with sensitivity and intelligence. But that the spirits of tradition and modernity should *both* make me unhappy, I found utterly inadmissible. The book in my hand suddenly called to mind my erstwhile nom de plume, Yoshi Juryō. The name was borrowed from a Chinese story by Master Han Fei, which told how a young boy, having travelled to Handan to learn how people walked there, had to crawl back on hands and knees, like a reptile, having forgotten they walked in Shouling. To see me now, anyone would have thought me every bit the "Young Man of Shouling", but to have taken on that pseudonym even before I fell into my present hell . . . Endeavouring to brush off these thoughts tormenting me, I turned my back on the large bookcase and stepped into the room directly opposite, where there was a poster display. But even there, right in the middle of one of the posters, I saw a knight in the form of St George slaying a winged dragon. Worse still, the contorted face looking out from under the helmet resembled a certain enemy of mine. Again I recalled Han Fei and one of his tales about the art of slaying dragons. Rather than continuing through the exhibition, I left via the broad staircase.

Night had fallen. As I walked along Nihonbashi-dōri I kept thinking about those words: "slaying dragons". This was, word for word, the inscription on an inkstone that I owned. It had been a gift from a certain young businessman, who after a long succession of failed business ventures had finally declared bankruptcy at the end of the previous year. I looked up to the lofty heavens to remind myself how small the world was—and, consequently, how small I myself was—amid the twinkling of countless stars. But after a full day of clear weather, the night sky had clouded over. Suddenly I felt the presence of some malign force watching over me and decided to take refuge in a café on the other side of the tram tracks.

This place was indeed a refuge. The rose-coloured walls of the café exuded a sense of peace and tranquillity. I took a seat at one of the tables in the rear. Fortunately, there were few customers other than me. I sipped a cup of cocoa and lit a customary cigarette, the smoke from which rose in faint blue curls up the pink walls. The gentle harmony of the colours was another source of pleasure for me. Before long, however, I spied on the wall to my left a portrait of Napoleon and soon enough the feeling of unease returned to me. As a student, Napoleon had inscribed in the last page of his geography book: "*Sainte-Hélène, petite île.*" This may well have been, as we say, a coincidence, but the memory must surely have provoked terror in him years later . . .

As I sat there, staring at Napoleon, I thought of the works I had written. The first to drift into mind was "Words of a Dwarf" and its aphorisms—particularly the line, "Life is more hellish than Hell itself." Then it was the fate of my artist Yoshihide, the protagonist of "Hell Screen". Next came . . . To escape these memories, I surveyed the café's interior as I puffed away at my cigarette. Not five minutes had passed since I sought shelter here, but in that brief time the café had undergone a stark transformation. What unnerved me most was the total lack of harmony between the imitation-mahogany furniture and the rose colour of the walls. Fearing another descent into an anguish known only to myself, I threw down a silver coin and hastily began to leave.

"Excuse me! Excuse me, sir! That'll be twenty sen . . ."

When I looked, I saw that the coin I had produced was copper.

I was walking down the street, feeling deeply humiliated, when thoughts suddenly sprang to mind of a home in a distant pine forest. This was not the home of my adoptive parents somewhere in the suburbs of Tokyo, but the house I was renting for myself and my family. I had been living in a house like that for a good ten years, but certain circumstances had led me rashly to take up residence again with my parents, thus transforming me instantly into a slave, a tyrant, a powerless egoist . . .

It was getting on for ten o'clock by the time I returned to the hotel. After all the walking I had done, I lacked the strength to go back to my room, and so I collapsed into a chair in the lobby, in front of a fire-place with copious burning logs. There, I set to think-ing about the historical novel I had been planning to write. It would string together some thirty-odd episodes in chronological order, with folk protagonists of every era, from Suiko right through to Meiji. As I watched the sparks fly in the fire, I suddenly found

myself thinking of a bronze statue outside the imperial palace. The figure wore armour and sat high
astride a horse, the very personification of loyalty. And
yet his enemies were—

"Lies!"

Once more I slipped from the distant past to the
immediate present. Fortunately, just then, there
happened along an older schoolmate, now a sculptor.
He was wearing his inevitable velvet jacket and sporting a short goatee. I rose from my chair and shook his
outstretched hand. (This was not my habit, although it
was his, he having lived half his life in Paris and Berlin.)
For some strange reason his hand was damp—like a
lizard's skin.

"Are you staying here?" he asked.

"I am, yes . . ."

"Work, is it?"

"Among other things."

He fixed me in his gaze. There was something
almost detective-like about his expression.

"Why don't you come up to my room for a chat?"
(I elected to take the offensive.) "How about it?"

This mercurial change in attitude, from customary
diffidence to sudden boldness, is one of my worse
traits.

"Lead the way," he said with a grin.

Shoulder to shoulder like the best of friends, we made our way through a group of softly spoken foreigners to my room. Once there, he sat down with his back to the mirror and started talking about all manner of things—although mostly about women. It was I who was paying for my sins in this hell, but the very fact made such talk of vice all the more depressing. Here was I, suddenly cast in the role of the puritan, heaping scorn on those women.

"Just look at the lips of S——ko. They've been kissed by any number of men, so many in fact that—"

I broke off mid-sentence, as I studied the reflection of his back in the mirror. There was a yellow plaster just below his ear.

"Any number of men, eh?"

"She certainly seems the sort."

He smiled and nodded. I felt him scrutinizing me, as though he were trying to learn my secrets. Still, we continued to dwell on the subject of women. Rather than despise him, however, I could not help but feel increasingly depressed and ashamed of my own frailties.

When at last he was gone, I lay out on the bed and began reading *A Dark Night's Passing*. Every last detail about the protagonist's psychological battle cut me to the quick. Next to this man, I felt like such an idiot that it brought tears to my eyes. The tears, in turn, afforded me a degree of peace—but that did not last for long. Once again, my right eye began to see semi-transparent cogwheels, and, once again, they multiplied as they went on turning. Fearing that my headache would return, I laid the book down by my pillow and took 800 mg of Veronal, determined to knock myself out.

I dreamt, however, that I was looking at a swimming pool, where a group of children, boys and girls, were splashing about in the water and diving below the water's surface. I turned my back on the pool and began walking towards the pine forest across the way. As I did, somebody's voice called out from behind me: "Papa!" I looked round to see my wife standing beside the pool, and in that moment I was struck by an intense feeling of regret.

"Papa, don't you want your towel?"

"I don't need it. Take care of the children!"

I carried on walking, but now the scene had changed into a railway platform. The station looked as though it was somewhere in the countryside; there was a long hedge running the length of the platform. There was also a university student by the name of H—— and an old lady. As soon as they saw me, they came over, both talking at the same time.

"Wasn't it a terrific fire?"

"I barely made it out of there."

I thought I had seen the old woman somewhere before. What's more, I felt a certain thrill in talking to her. At that point, a train glided up to the platform amid clouds of smoke. I was the only one to get on. I passed down the gangway of the wagon-lit; on both sides, white sheets hung from the berths. On one of them lay, almost like a mummy, the naked body of a woman facing towards me. It was my goddess of vengeance again, my Fury—the madman's daughter . . .

I awoke and leapt out of bed. The electric light made my room seem unusually bright, but from somewhere I could hear the sound of wings and the squeaking of rats. I opened the door and rushed down the corridor to the fireplace. I sat down in front of it and began to watch the flickering flames. A porter in a white uniform approached with fresh firewood.

"What time is it?"

"I believe it's three-thirty, sir."

Despite the hour, there was a woman—most likely an American—sitting alone in a corner of the lobby, reading a book. Even from across the room, I could see that her dress was green. Feeling a kind of salvation, I resolved to sit there and wait for the night to end, like an old man who, after many years of painful suffering, quietly awaits his death . . .

4. MORE?

In my hotel room, at last, I managed to complete the story I had been writing and prepared to send it to a certain magazine. The honorarium I was to receive wouldn't cover even the bill for my week's stay in the hotel. Nevertheless, I still felt satisfied at having finished the work, and so I decided to head out to a bookshop in the Ginza to find a tonic for my soul.

Perhaps it was the quality of light, the golden winter sun, that gave the little scraps of paper strewn across the asphalt the appearance of rose petals. As I entered the bookshop, I was buoyed by a feeling of benevolence that seemed to be directed towards me. The shop, too, was somehow prettier than usual, but it was the sight of a young girl in spectacles talking to the shop assistant that troubled me. Even so, I recalled the paper rose petals scattered in the street and made up my mind to buy *Conversations with Anatole France* and *The Collected Letters of Prosper Mérimée*.

Carrying both volumes under my arm, I went into a café, took a table right at the very back, and waited for my coffee to come. Opposite me sat a couple, probably a mother and son. The boy was younger than I, but our resemblance was uncanny. What was more, the two of them were chatting like lovers, their faces pressed close together. Watching them, I realized that the son, at least, was conscious of how much erotic pleasure he was giving his mother. This was undoubtedly a classic example of the sheer power of human attraction, with which I had some familiarity. It was also a classic example of a certain will that transforms this world of ours into a veritable hell. And yet . . .

The fortuitous arrival of my coffee spared me another descent into the anguish I so feared and started me reading the Mérimée book. His letters were peppered with the same pithy aphorisms that glittered in his novels. Those aphorisms worked quickly to steel my nerves. (Being so easily influenced by such things was another weakness of mine.) Having drained my cup, I hastened out of the café, feeling that I could take on whatever came my way.

As I walked down the street, I studied the various window displays. One framer's shop had a portrait of Beethoven hanging there—a characteristic likeness of the genius with hair sticking out in all directions. I could not help feeling that there was something quite comical about it . . .

As I stood there, I was suddenly approached by an old friend from my high-school days, now a professor of applied chemistry. He was carrying a large brief-case and one of his eyes was bloodshot.

"What happened to your eye?"

"This? Oh, it's just conjunctivitis."

It suddenly occurred to me that over the past fifteen years, whenever I experienced that feeling of attraction, my eye would develop conjunctivitis, just like his. Of course, I said nothing about this. He clapped me on the shoulder and started talking about our mutual acquaintances. He was still going on when he led me into a café.

"It's certainly been a while," he said, lighting a cigar across the marble table. "The last time I saw you must have been at the unveiling of the Shu Shunsui monument."

"Yes. Shu Shun . . ."

For some reason I stumbled over the pronunciation. The experience disconcerted me, especially given that it was, after all, a Japanese name. My friend, however, paid no attention to it and just carried on talking about all manner of things—about the novelist K——, about the bulldog he had bought, about the poison gas Lewisite.

"You don't seem to have been writing much lately. I read your 'Death Register' though ... Is it autobiographical?"

"Yes, my autobiography."

"Morbid stuff. Are you feeling better these days?"

"Much as always. All I seem to do is take pills."

"I've been suffering from insomnia myself lately."

" 'Myself'? Why do you say 'myself'?"

"Well you're supposedly the insomniac, aren't you? It's a dangerous business, insomnia . . ."

Something like a smile flashed in his bloodshot left eye. Before I could reply, I had a premonition that I would be unable to pronounce the word "insomnia".

"What do you expect from the son of a madwoman . . ."

Not even ten minutes later, I found myself alone again, walking down the street. Some of the little scraps of paper littering the asphalt had now taken on the appearance of human faces. Just then, I happened to see a woman with bobbed hair coming towards me. From a distance she looked beautiful, but up close I could see that her face was lined and ugly. She also appeared to be pregnant. Instinctively, I averted my eyes and turned in to a side street. After a few minutes of walking, however, I felt my haemorrhoids begin to ache. The only remedy for the pain was a sitz bath. *Sitz baths: Beethoven himself used to take them . . .*

All of a sudden, my nostrils were assaulted by the stench of sulphur used in sitz baths, though there was, of course, no sulphur to be seen anywhere in the street. Thinking again of the paper rose petals, I tried as best I could to steady my gait.

An hour later I found myself shut away in my room, seated at the desk in front of the window and making a start on a new story. My pen raced over the manuscript paper with a speed that I found quite astonishing, but after two or three hours it came to a halt, as though stayed by some invisible force. Having no other recourse, I stood up and began pacing about the room. It was at times like this that my megalomania was at its most extreme. In my savage joy, I felt that I had no parents, no wife or children, but only the life that gushed forth from my pen.

Five minutes later, however, my attention was drawn to the telephone. No matter how many times I spoke after answering it, however, the receiver emitted only the same strange, indistinct word over and over. It seemed to be saying "more", or perhaps "mole". Eventually I abandoned the telephone and resumed pacing about the room. But at every step, I was hounded by this curious word.

"Mole . . ." I didn't like the association of the English word, but a few seconds later I recast it as the French *mort*, "death"—and with it a new wave of anxiety washed over me. Death seemed to be bearing down on me just as it had done to my sister's husband. And yet, in spite of my anxious state, I found myself strangely amused. Before I knew it, I was smiling. Why? Where had this come from? I had no idea. For the first time in quite some while I stood before the mirror, face-to-face with my reflection. Naturally, my reflection was smiling back at me. As I stared at him, I thought about my other self, my double. Fortunately, I had never seen my double—or what the Germans call a *Doppelgänger*. However, the wife of my friend K——, who was now a film actor in America, had seen my double in a corridor at the Imperial Theatre. (I recalled my confusion when K——'s wife said to me out of the blue, "I'm sorry I didn't have a chance to say hello the other night.") And then there was the time when a certain one-legged translator, now deceased, had seen him in a tobacconist's in the Ginza. Perhaps Death was coming for my double and not for me. But then, even if he was coming for me . . . Turning my back to the mirror, I returned to my desk by the window.

The square window, framed in volcanic stone, looked out onto a withered lawn and a pond. As I gazed at this garden scene, I thought about all the notebooks and the unfinished play I had burned in that distant pine forest. Then, taking up my pen, I set to work again on my new story.

5. RED LIGHTS

Sunlight had begun to torment me. A mole indeed, I drew the curtain across the window and kept the electric light burning as I pressed on with my story. Whenever I tired of writing, I would open Taine's *Histoire de la littérature anglaise* and peruse his lives of the poets. They were each, without exception, unhappy men. Even the masters of the Elizabethan age . . . Ben Jonson, the greatest scholar of his day, succumbed to such nervous exhaustion that he found himself witnessing the armies of Rome and Carthage doing battle on his big toe. I could not resist a cruel, swelling sense of glee at their misfortunes.

One night when a strong east wind was blowing (a lucky omen), I ventured out through the basement and into the street, in search of a certain old man. He worked as the caretaker of a bible publishing house, where he lived alone in the attic, devoting himself to prayer and scripture. Beneath a crucifix on the wall we warmed our hands by the brazier and talked of many things. Why had my mother gone mad? Why had my father's business failed? Why was I again being punished? He alone knew the answers to these mysteries and, always wearing a strangely solemn smile, would keep me company until all hours of the night. Sometimes he would paint, in a few short words, a caricature of human life. I could not help but feel respect for this attic-dwelling hermit. Yet, as we talked, I discovered that he too was capable of being moved by the force of attraction.

"The gardener's daughter is a pretty little thing, and such a sweet girl . . . She's awfully good to me."

"How old?"

"She'll be eighteen this year."

Perhaps, to him, his love for the girl was paternal. But I couldn't help noticing the passion in his eyes. And on the yellowing skin of the apple he offered me, there appeared the outline of a *kirin*. (I was often finding mythological creatures in the grain of wood or in the cracks of coffee cups.) That it was a *kirin* I could tell conclusively from the single horn it had. Recalling the time when a hostile critic had dubbed me "the *kirin* child of the 1910s", I realized that even here in this attic, under the cross, I had no safe haven.

"How have you been lately?" he asked.

"Same as ever. On the edge, nerves frayed."

"The drugs won't help you. Have you no inclination towards faith?"

"If only I had . . ."

"It isn't difficult, you know. All you have to do is believe in God, in His son Jesus Christ, and in the miracles that He worked . . ."

"I can believe in the Devil . . ."

"Then why not God? If you believe in shadows, then you must also believe in light."

"But there is darkness without light."

"Darkness without light?"

I was at a loss for something to say. He too was walking through the darkness, just as I was. Though he believed in light as well as darkness. This was the only point on which our logic differed. And yet, for me at least, the gulf between us was unbridgeable . . .

"But there must be light," he insisted. "The miracles prove it . . . Even in our own times, miracles do happen."

"Those worked by the Devil, maybe . . ."

"Why dwell on the Devil?"

I was tempted to tell him of all the trials I had undergone during these past few years, but I was afraid that word might find its way from him to my family and, like my mother, that I should end up in a mental asylum.

"What's that you have there?" I asked.

The vigorous old man turned to his ageing book-shelves, with something of a Pan-like look on his face.

"The complete works of Dostoevsky. Have you ever read *Crime and Punishment?*"

I had, of course, acquainted myself with four or five volumes of Dostoevsky a decade earlier, but what struck me was his incidental mention (or was it?) of that particular title, and so I asked him to lend it to me before I went back to my hotel. The crowded streets, resplendent in electric light, were as distressing as ever. To run into an acquaintance now would have been utterly unbearable. Where I could, I opted, like a thief in the night, to take only the darkest streets.

Soon enough, however, I began to notice a pain in my stomach, for which the only remedy was a glass of whisky. I found a bar and, giving the door a push, stepped inside. In the cramped, smoke-filled place stood a group of youths—artists, probably—engaged in drinking. They were gathered around a woman whose hair covered her ears in the latest fashion, and who was applying herself passionately to the mando-lin. It was all too much for me, and so I immediately turned back and walked out the door. It was then I discovered that my shadow was swaying from side to side and that I was bathed in an eerie red light. I stopped in my tracks, but, just as before, my shadow kept moving. With fear and trepidation, I looked up and discovered at last the coloured glass lantern hanging from the eaves of the bar, swaying heavily in the fierce wind . . .

The next place I tried was a basement restaurant. I went up to the bar and ordered a glass of whisky.

"Whisky? All we have is Black and White, sir . . ."

I cut my whisky with soda water and began sipping it in silence. Beside me sat two men in their late twenties or early thirties, newspaper journalists to all appearances. They were discussing something in hushed tones—and in French. Although I kept my back to them, I could feel them looking me over from head to toe. Their gaze transmitted to my body like radio waves. They knew my name, that much was certain, and they seemed to be gossiping about me . . .

"*Bien . . . très mauvais . . . pourquoi? . . .*"

"*Pourquoi? . . . le diable est mort! . . .*"

"*Oui, oui . . . d'enfer . . .*"

I threw down a silver coin (my last one) on the bar and fled this underground room. The street, swept by the night wind, helped to steady my nerves, now that my stomach ache had eased off. I thought of Raskolnikov and felt the desire to confess everything, but that would be sure to result in tragedy for others besides me, besides even my family. Not only that, but I couldn't be sure that the desire itself was genuine. If only I had the steady nerves of someone normal. But for that to happen, I'd have to go somewhere—to Madrid, to Rio, to Samarkand . . .

Not long after that, I was alarmed by the unexpected sight of a small white signboard hanging from the eaves of a shop. It was emblazoned with a trademark: an automobile tyre with wings. It made me think of the ancient Greek who placed his faith in artificial wings. He soared up high into the sky, until his wings were burnt by the sun and he went plunging into the ocean, where he drowned. To Madrid, to Rio, to Samarkand . . . I had to laugh at these reveries. But at the same time, I could not banish the thought of Orestes pursued by the Furies.

I followed the dark path along the canal. I found myself recalling the suburban house of my adoptive parents. They were bound to be hoping for my return each day. Very probably my children, too . . . But I feared the force that would inevitably fetter me the moment I set foot in there. On the rippling surface of the canal, a barge was moored, a faint light stealing out from below deck. Even in a place like this, no doubt, families, men and women, were living, hating one another in order to love one another . . . But now, though still feeling the effects of the whisky, I summoned my fighting spirit once more and decided to return to my hotel.

At the desk I continued reading Mérimée's letters and, before I knew it, I found that they had given me the strength to go on living. When I learnt, however, that in his twilight years Mémirée had converted to Protestantism, I felt as though I were seeing for the first time the face behind the mask. He, too, was some-one who had walked through the darkness. Through the darkness? Now *A Dark Night's Passing* took on a terrifying significance for me. To allay my melancholy, I picked up *Conversations with Anatole France*, but this latter-day Pan, too, had his cross to bear . . .

Barely an hour had passed when the porter dropped by to deliver a bundle of letters. One of them was from a publisher in Leipzig, asking whether I would write an essay on "the modern Japanese woman". Why should he approach me, of all people, with a request like that, I wondered. The letter, in English, was followed by a handwritten postscript: "*A straightforward black-and-white portrait, in the style of a Japanese ink painting, would also suit our purposes.*" This line put me in mind of the Black and White whisky I had drunk earlier, and so I tore the letter to pieces. I opened another envelope at random and ran my eyes over the missive written on yellow letter paper. The young correspondent was unknown to me, but no sooner had I reached the second or third line than the words "... your 'Hell Screen' ..." somewhat predictably unnerved me. The third one I opened contained a letter from my nephew. With a sigh of relief, I could at last turn my attention to family affairs. But even this delivered an unexpected blow in the end:

"I'm sending you the reprint of Saitō's *Red Lights* ..."

Red lights! Sensing that I was being mocked, I fled the room, seeking refuge outside it. Not a soul was in the corridor. Propping myself against the wall, I made my way to the lobby, where I sat down in an armchair and decided to permit myself a cigarette. For some inexplicable reason, however, the cigarettes were branded Airship. (Since arriving at this hotel, I had smoked nothing but Star cigarettes.) Once again, my eyes were confronted with the sight of artificial wings. I summoned a porter and asked for two packs of Star. If the porter was to be trusted, they had run out of Star.

"We do have Airship, though, sir."

I shook my head and surveyed the vast lobby. Across from me, four or five foreigners were sitting around a table. One of them—a woman in a red dress—kept glancing my way, it seemed, while she and her companions exchanged words in hushed tones.

"Mrs Townshead . . ." some invisible voice whispered to me.

Naturally, I didn't know any Mrs Townshead. Supposing even that it was the name of the woman sitting over there . . .

I got up from the chair and, fearing the onset of madness, decided to return to my room.

It had been my intention to telephone the mental hospital immediately, but I knew that my being admitted to that place would be a death sentence. After much indecision, and to dispel my fear, I began reading *Crime and Punishment*. The page to which I turned at random, however, was a passage from *The Brothers Karamazov*. Had I picked up the wrong book? I looked at the cover. *Crime and Punishment*—there was no doubting it, the book was *Crime and Punishment*. There must have been a binding error at the publishing house . . . That the binder had included pages from the wrong book, and that I, moreover, had opened the book at those very pages, revealed, I thought, the finger of Fate at work. Despite myself, I read on. Scarcely had I managed a page when a shudder ran through my whole body. It was the passage describing how Ivan was tormented by the Devil. Ivan, Strindberg, Maupassant, and now, here in this room, I myself . . .

My only salvation now was sleep. But I didn't have a single sleeping pill left. The grim prospect of more insomnia was utterly intolerable, but still, mustering a sort of desperate courage, I ordered coffee to be brought to the room and, like one demented, took up my pen. Two pages, five, seven, ten pages—the manuscript kept growing before my very eyes. I was filling the world of this novel with supernatural beasts, one of which was a self-portrait. But all of a sudden, fatigue began to cloud my head. At last I got up from the desk and lay down on the bed. I must have slept for forty or fifty minutes, when again I heard a voice whispering to me:

"*Le diable est mort.*"

I woke with a jolt and stood up. On the other side of the window with its volcanic stone, night was giving way to a cold dawn. I stood directly against the door and examined the empty room. Clouded over in parts by condensation, the glass windowpane opposite me revealed a miniature landscape: a tawny pine forest facing the sea. With trepidation, I drew nearer to the window, only to discover that the features of the landscape were, in reality, nothing more than the garden's withered lawn and the pond. But still, the illusion had inspired in me a longing akin to homesickness.

As I stuffed my books and the manuscript into the satchel on the desk, I made a decision: as soon as the clock stuck nine, I would place a call to a certain magazine and, one way or another, arrange for some money. Then I would go home.

6. AEROPLANE

I found myself in a taxi, racing from a station on the Tōkaidō line to my home in a seaside resort. For some reason, in spite of the cold, the driver had only an old raincoat draped over his shoulders. This coincidence was unsettling. So as not to look at him, I tried to keep my eyes trained out the window. What I saw was a funeral procession passing by some low-lying pines, probably on the old highway. I couldn't make out any of the usual white funerary lanterns or dragon lamps, but there were artificial lotus flowers of gold and silver swaying gently at either end of the palanquin . . .

Home at last, I spent the next few days in relative peace, thanks to my wife and children—and thanks also to the efficacy of barbiturates. From my upstairs study, I could look out over the tops of the pine trees to the distant sea beyond. I had decided to work at my desk only in the mornings, with the cooing of pigeons in my ears. In addition to pigeons and crows, sparrows too visited the veranda. This was another source of pleasure for me. Pen in hand, I would think of the words: "A lucky sparrow enters the chamber . . ."

One overcast, muggy afternoon I ventured out to buy ink at a variety shop. The only kind they had, however, was sepia—the one colour that has always unnerved me. Having no alternative, I left the shop and went for a solitary stroll among the deserted streets. A swaggering foreigner, fortyish and apparently myopic, happened to come my way. He was the local Swede, who suffered from a persecution complex and whose name was actually Strindberg. As we passed, I felt a physical jolt.

The street was only a couple of blocks long, but in the time that it took me to walk the length of it the same dog passed me four times. Half its face was black. As I turned down a side street, I recalled the Black and White whisky—and that Strindberg's tie had also been black and white. That this could have been a mere coincidence was unthinkable. And yet, if wasn't a coincidence . . . I stopped momentarily in the middle of the street and felt as if my mind were still walking on ahead. On the roadside, behind a wire fence, a glass bowl lay discarded. It had a faint rainbow-hued shimmer to it, and around the base, in relief, was a design of bird's wings. Just then several sparrows swooped down to it from the tops of the pine trees, but no sooner had they reached the bowl than together they soared up again into the sky . . .

I went to my wife's family home and sat down in a rattan chair on the veranda overlooking the garden. Inside a wire-mesh enclosure at the back of the garden, several white leghorns were quietly strutting around. At my feet lay another black dog. Even as I grappled with unanswerable riddles, I carried on a show of cool chatter with my mother-in-law and my wife's younger brother.

"It's certainly peaceful here, isn't it?"

"Only by Tokyo standards."

"Oh? Are there noisy goings-on here too?"

"Well, it's no idyll, if that's what you mean," my mother-in-law laughed. And indeed, she was right: this place was no idyll. I knew only too well what sins and tragedies had gone on here in the space of one short year. The doctor who was bent on slowly poisoning his patients, the old woman who had set fire to the home of her adopted son and his wife, the lawyer who had sought to strip his younger sister of her assets . . . For me, seeing the houses of these people was nothing short of witnessing a living hell.

"You have a madman living around here, don't you?"

"Oh, you mean young H——? He isn't mad. He's just an imbecile."

"I'm sure he's schizophrenic. I always have this eerie feeling whenever I see him. It's unbearable. Just the other day, I saw him bowing to the Horsehead Kannon."

"An eerie feeling? Well I never . . . You ought to toughen up."

"He's tougher than I am . . ." ventured my brother-in-law in his usual hesitant manner. He was sitting up on his futon, his face darkened by several days' stubble.

"Strength also has its weaknesses . . ."

"Good grief, what are we to say to *that*?"

I couldn't suppress a wry smile as I looked at my mother-in-law. My wife's brother was smiling too. As he gazed at the pine forest beyond the far hedge, he carried on talking distractedly. (Often this young convalescent looked to me the very image of a spirit having escaped the flesh.)

"To think, one minute you can be so detached from the world around, and the next, at the mercy of violent human passions . . ."

"To think, man can be virtuous one moment, and wicked the next."

"No, it's something more antithetical than good and evil . . ."

"Like a man who finds the child within himself?"

"No, not that either. I can't find the words for it, but . . . Perhaps it's like poles of electricity, having two opposites in one."

The fearsome noise of an aeroplane startled us. I instinctively looked up at the sky and saw it climbing up after almost clipping the tops of the pine trees. An unusual model, it had a single set of wings painted yellow. The chickens, also startled by the noise, scattered in all directions, while the dog in particular began to bark and, with its tail between its legs, took shelter under the veranda.

"That aeroplane could crash."

"No, it'll be fine . . . By the way, have you ever heard of aeroplane sickness?"

Instead of answering with a verbal "no", I shook my head as I lit a cigarette.

"They say that people who fly in planes like that get so used to breathing in the high-altitude air that eventually they find they can't bear to breathe the air down here anymore . . ."

Having left my mother-in-law's house behind, I took a walk through the perfect stillness of the pine forest, falling steadily into a depression. Why had that aeroplane flown over my head and not somebody else's? Why did the hotel have only Airship cigarettes? Plagued by these questions, I chose a deserted path and set off down it.

The sea beyond the low-lying sand dunes stretched out, ashen in its cloudy reflections. A swing set with no swing jutted up from one of the dunes. As I gazed at it, I immediately thought of the gallows. There were even a couple of crows perching on top of it. They watched me but gave no sign of flight. On the contrary: the one in the middle raised its large beak heavenward and cawed precisely four times.

I had been walking along a sandbank with withered grass, but now chose to turn down a narrow lane lined with villas. Somewhere on the right, among the tall pines, there ought to have been the white gleam of a two-storey wooden building in the Western style (an old friend of mine had dubbed it "The House of Spring"). But when I reached the spot where it was supposed to be, all that remained was a bathtub standing on a concrete plinth. *Fire*—I immediately thought before walking on, trying to avert my eyes. Just then, I saw a man on a bicycle coming right at me. He had on an olive-brown flat cap and was hunched over the handlebars, his eyes, strangely, fixed straight ahead. I had the fleeting impression that I recognized in the man's face that of my sister's husband, but I turned down a small side lane before he was close enough for me to tell. Right in the middle of that lane, however, lay the rotting corpse of a mole lying belly-up.

Someone was stalking me. With every step I took, my feeling of apprehension grew. Then, one by one, semi-transparent cogwheels began to block my field of vision. Terrified that my final moments were drawing near, I walked on with my head held erect. The number of wheels increased, and they began to spin ever faster. At the same time, the pines to my right, with their unmoving, intertwined branches, began to look as if I were seeing them through finely cut glass. I could feel my heart beating faster; several times I tried to pause by the side of the road, but someone seemed to be urging me on, preventing me from stopping . . .

Half an hour later, I found myself at home again, lying on my back upstairs, my eyes tightly shut as I endured a violent headache. Just then, behind my eyelids I began to see a single wing with silver feathers overlapped like fish scales. The image was projected onto my retina with such flawless clarity. I opened my eyes and looked up at the ceiling. Having made sure that there was no such image there, I closed them again. But there again was that silver wing, reflected perfectly in the dark. All of a sudden, I remembered having seen a wing on the radiator cap of a taxi I had recently taken . . .

Someone came clattering up the stairs before crashing back down again. Realizing that that "someone" was my wife, I got up in alarm and hurried down to poke my head into the gloomy sitting room at the bottom of the stairs. I found my wife lying flat out on the floor, gasping for breath, her shoulders heaving.

"What's wrong?"

"It's nothing, I'm fine . . ."

At last my wife managed to lift her head and give me a forced smile. "I don't know why," she continued, "but for some reason I just had this feeling that you were about to die . . ."

This was the most terrifying experience of my life—

I haven't the strength to go on writing this. To live in this state of mind is an agony beyond all words. Isn't there someone kind enough to strangle me softly in my sleep?

PUSHKIN PRESS

Pushkin Press was founded in 1997, and publishes novels, essays, memoirs, children's books—everything from timeless classics to the urgent and contemporary.

This book is part of the Pushkin Collection of paperbacks, designed to be as satisfying as possible to hold and to enjoy. It is typeset in Monotype Baskerville, based on the transitional English serif typeface designed in the mid-eighteenth century by John Baskerville. It was litho-printed on Munken Premium White Paper and notch-bound by the independently owned printer TJ International in Padstow, Cornwall. The cover, with French flaps, was printed on Rives Linear Bright White paper. The paper and cover board are both acid-free and Forest Stewardship Council (FSC) certified.

Pushkin Press publishes the best writing from around the world—great stories, beautifully produced, to be read and read again.

STEFAN ZWEIG · EDGAR ALLAN POE · ISAAC BABEL
TOMÁS GONZÁLEZ · ULRICH PLENZDORF · JOSEPH KESSEL
VELIBOR ČOLIĆ · LOUISE DE VILMORIN · MARCEL AYMÉ
ALEXANDER PUSHKIN · MAXIM BILLER · JULIEN GRACQ
BROTHERS GRIMM · HUGO VON HOFMANNSTHAL
GEORGE SAND · PHILIPPE BEAUSSANT · IVÁN REPILA
E.T.A. HOFFMANN · ALEXANDER LERNET-HOLENIA
YASUSHI INOUE · HENRY JAMES · FRIEDRICH TORBERG
ARTHUR SCHNITZLER · ANTOINE DE SAINT-EXUPÉRY
MACHI TAWARA · GAITO GAZDANOV · HERMANN HESSE
LOUIS COUPERUS · JAN JACOB SLAUERHOFF
PAUL MORAND · MARK TWAIN · PAUL FOURNEL
ANTAL SZERB · JONA OBERSKI · MEDARDO FRAILE
HÉCTOR ABAD · PETER HANDKE · ERNST WEISS
PENELOPE DELTA · RAYMOND RADIGUET · PETR KRÁL
ITALO SVEVO · RÉGIS DEBRAY · BRUNO SCHULZ · TEFFI
EGON HOSTOVSKÝ · JOHANNES URZIDIL · JÓZEF WITTLIN